Sweet Attraction

LOVE HAPPENS • BOOK ONE

SUSAN WARNER

Copyright © 2019 Susan Warner

All rights reserved.

Without limiting the rights under copyright preserved above, no part of this book may be reproduced, stored in or introduced into a retrieval system, or transmitted, in any form, or by any means, (electronic, mechanical, photocopying, recording, or otherwise), without the prior written permission of both the copyright holder and the publisher of this book.

This is a work of fiction. Names, characters, places, and incidents either are the product of the author's imagination or are used fictitiously, and any resemblance to actual persons, living or dead, business establishments, events, or locales is entirely coincidental.

First Edition. May 5, 2019

Sweet Attraction

Prologue

Seventeen years earlier

"If you want to be with them so bad, go to them and see if they take you in! You'll be back before the sun comes up!"

Seventeen-year-old Ethan Young shielded his head as two pairs of jeans were thrown at him, along with his shirts. He didn't answer this taunt his father hurled at him from the front door. No matter what his father, Barrick Young, said to him, Ethan always held his tongue. It was hard sometimes, but his father had taught him well. Barrick had said on more than one occasion, "When you feel as though you know more than me, you're free to pack up your belongings and prove it. Outside of my house."

His father seemed to be making good on that promise tonight. Ethan didn't flinch when the door slammed, leaving him in the dark on the front porch. The dark didn't matter to him though, and he thought it was fitting that a cool breeze was coming through this night.

He had grown up in Sweet Blooms, Florida, but if anyone in town was asked, they would say Ethan lived on the outskirts. The outskirts were the unattractive pieces of land that were barely farmable and usually bordered on at least two sides by swamp. He knew how close he was from gator space, and he was always aware of and looking for the glassy reflection of eyes. Without his shotgun though, seeing that telltale sign might be too late. Good thing he had no intentions of sleeping out in front of the house.

Instead, he felt for his pants and shirts. He tossed them over his shoulder and proceeded to do just what his father had taught him. He was going to prove that he knew what he was doing.

The people in town always looked down their noses when he and his father came around, and in truth, Ethan couldn't blame them. His father never wanted to go into town until after they had done their fishing or farming on the small plot of land they had. When they'd go, they were smelly from the day's work and had more dirt on them than anything else. He'd always told him the townspeople shouldn't be ashamed of people who work.

Ethan loved his dad. He didn't know all the details, but he knew that his dad had taken care of him the best he could when his mother went away. He knew Barrick wasn't the smartest man, but he had a good heart and he worked hard. With very few exceptions, Barrick didn't talk to anyone, so he had no griefs with anyone.

Ethan was grateful for all his dad had given to him and given up for him. But tonight, they had turned a corner neither one of them could un-turn. Ethan Young was in love. He didn't expect his dad to understand because the girl he loved was Lydia Mason. Barrick had told him more than once; Lydia Mason was the mayor's daughter. Lydia Mason was going places and her mother would never approve of Ethan. He told him if Lydia had to choose Ethan would be alone.

Ethan hadn't told Lydia about his feelings, and they hadn't been going out or anything. At the end of the day, he had nothing to offer her.

Lydia was pretty. She had hair like corn silk, and she was incredibly smart. When he went to school, she tutored him in math, and she made it all make sense. She didn't get offended by his worn clothing or his not-so-fresh smell. His father had told him to look for a person's character, and it would shine through. Ethan saw Lydia's character, and she was a beacon for all to see.

Ethan had received an acceptance letter to a nearby school. He hadn't told his father because every time he brought up college, his dad said it was a waste.

He would toss out things like, "You don't need no paper to farm." Or, "Getting a piece of paper won't change what you are in Sweet Blooms. Once from the outskirts, always from the outskirts."

Ethan dreamed of someplace other than Sweet Blooms. He was tired of rolling hills, uniformly planted farms, and a town that looked like it hadn't been touched by time. People still made milkshakes by hand. The bakery was run by three women, named after flowers, who never seemed to age. Everyone knew everyone in town. He couldn't introduce himself to anyone, they all knew him and had an expectation.

He was Barrick's son. He would always live on the outskirts. He would do exactly what his dad had done before him.

Tonight, Ethan gathered his clothes and made his way to his second truck, which he'd rebuilt from parts. He was making a change. As he got in his truck and turned the key, the truck stalled. He laid his head on the steering wheel and took a couple of deep breaths.

He turned the key again.

Again, it stalled.

The door to the house opened, and Ethan could see his father's silhouette in the door. Ethan turned the key again. He just needed it to start. Here he was making his great exit, and his truck wouldn't start. His body tensed as he saw his dad step out of the house and walk toward him.

Would he tell him *I told you so*? Would he listen to the truck and tell him it was a sign from above that he was being silly? Ethan didn't know, but the burn of unshed tears of frustration threatened to fall.

His father was standing in front of the truck in the headlights. Barrick was a big, burly man with wide shoulders. He knew when others looked at him that all they saw was brawn and no brains.

When Ethan looked at him, he saw the man who carried him on his shoulders and told him to try and catch a star. Ethan saw the man who took him to a diner when a girl stood him up because she wouldn't be seen with a boy from the outskirts. He saw a man who taught him that hard work was something to be proud of.

Tonight, he was trying to leave him and be his own person.

His dad hit the top of the truck twice. Ethan reacted on habit and opened the hood. His dad was under the hood for maybe three minutes. Then Barrick closed the hood and gave him a nod. Ethan reached for the key with a trembling hand. He turned the key, and the engine started.

Barrick walked up to Ethan on the driver side. Ethan didn't have to worry about lowering the window—there wasn't one.

"You leaving?" Barrick asked.

"Yes, pop. I need—"

"I don't have what you need, Ethan. That's a heck of a realization for a father to come to."

Ethan was speechless.

"Pop, it's not you, it's just that I want—"

"More?"

Ethan sighed and nodded yes.

Barrick ran his hand through his hair. Then he looked into the darkness behind the truck before turning back to Ethan. Ethan could see his pop's expression had changed. If there had been any softening in his feelings or thoughts a few moments ago, it would have been part of Ethan's imagination. Now his father had the look of a man who was ready to go to battle.

"Go then. I didn't have enough to keep your mother, and it looks like I'm not enough to keep you either."

Those were the final words Barrick Young said to his son, and he turned and went back into the house. Ethan stayed in the same place until the door was slammed shut behind his dad and he was sitting in the darkness. Again. It took him a moment to realize there were tears running down his face. When he did, Ethan wiped them away and drove off.

He'd come home one day. He wouldn't be Barrick Young's son. He'd be Ethan Young. He'd be someone his dad would be proud of, and hopefully someone he would be able to forgive.

One

"Really? It's the age of computers, who needs all of these binders?"

Lydia Mason tried to climb up the courthouse steps. It was a beautiful day. That wasn't really saying anything, though. It was always relatively beautiful in Sweet Blooms. Today Lydia had her hair in a bun, and she wore a black suit that could be business appropriate but was also funeral appropriate, if need be. She followed up her ensemble with a pair of non-matching navy-blue three-inch heels. All of which didn't matter because Sweet Blooms' most recent law graduate was tottering up the stairs carrying green bar paper binders to her mother, who just happened to be the mayor of Sweet Blooms.

As she struggled to keep the stacked books in her arms, she took little breaths. "Don't even think about falling, you pile of repurposed firewood," Lydia mumbled, slowly going up the steps. If her count was right, she had five more steps to go.

Then it happened like the last scene in a tragic story as if her fate had been choreographed while she slept, when she lifted her foot to put it on the next step, her heel got caught, and she wobbled.

"You will not be outdoing the leader of the gymnastics team, you pile of confetti," Lydia said, then she realigned her body and prayed no one was behind her to see her make that adjustment. Just when she was sure she had her footing; she heard a voice from behind her.

"I'll be right there, hold on," a man called. "Don't move."

Lydia leaned her head on the pile in her arms. "White knights," she muttered. "Why do they always think I need help?"

Lydia turned her head to the side and tried to yell over her shoulder. "I'm good, don't bother."

"You're not—the books are sliding to the right," the man insisted.

"Of course, they are, because my head turned to the right to call over my shoulder. I'm correcting it now."

Lydia turned her head back to the front and once again started her ascent. She made sure her foot was squarely on the next step before she moved. It was obviously too quick because the books wobbled in her arms.

"Come on, Lydia, you've got four more steps to go."

"I'm right here to help you," the guy stated.

Lydia jumped when she heard how close he was. If she thought she could do it, she'd give him a mule kick for startling her. On second thought, she wouldn't. She'd just glued that heel back on two days ago; testing it against a grown man was not the way to go.

"Back away," she said. "I'm almost at the top. Don't mess up my balance."

"I'm here to help your balance."

The comment was so ludicrous, she turned her head too quickly to address it. The move was just enough to push the books to the side, tilting her as well. She planted her feet to try and correct herself. It was then she felt the shift in her glued-on heel and was completely thrown off balance.

Lydia heard the billowing pages as they fell to the ground. She put her hands out to catch herself. Instead of falling onto the steps as she had anticipated, she slammed into the unknown guy.

Safely in his arms, she looked at the books on the ground. Some were open, some were closed, and a couple of the papers looked like they hadn't fared too badly. All of this would have never happened if it weren't for the solid guy who was holding her. She pushed away from him and then pulled her jacket down to make herself presentable. Lydia then turned to do battle with the one who wouldn't listen.

"Listen Mr.—" Lydia stopped midsentence. This wasn't someone trying to do something nice for the Mayor's daughter. He also wasn't someone who needed her to be lenient in a court case. Mister Tall Dark and Handsome—city style—was a hotshot realtor from New York who wouldn't leave her alone. He had to be hiding behind those glasses. Did anyone even wear glasses anymore? He also had a fashionable beard that was well kept.

Ethan Young, realtor extraordinaire. His smiling face was on tons of magazine ads and billboards that advertised the best places and the most anticipated new communities. All of his pictures had been headshots, but she could now attest that his body was just as trim and well put together as his headshots made him look. He was looking at her with concern on his face, and it made him more endearing than his smile. When this man focused on a woman, she was surely envied by many.

She recalled that he'd called her a few times, wanting to talk about the future of Sweet Blooms. He'd been persistent in suggesting that Sweet Blooms could use some additional income, and he wanted to discuss it with her. She had ended those calls as quickly as she politely could. She hadn't wanted to talk about it with him, but she also hadn't wanted to be rude.

In truth, she had to admit that his calls had made her look into the town books and even talk to her mother. Both inquiries supported Mr. Young's claims. Sweet Blooms needed money. The cost had grown, but the average income of Sweet Blooms hadn't, and it was becoming harder and harder to provide upgrades and services that were becoming mandatory.

"Hello, Ms. Mason," he said with a smile. "I'm glad to be here to save you."

Lydia looked at him incredulously. "What are you talking about? I hope your real estate deals are more thought-out than that statement you just made."

One side of his mouth tilted up. "So, it would be too much to think you were about to say thank you to me?"

Lydia took a step away from him, wiggling the foot with the glued heel to make sure it was still secured. Then she crossed her arms and looked at the mess on the steps. "I've heard about your positive thinking, but you're taking it to new levels."

Ethan laughed. "I think that is the politest way I've ever heard someone tell me that I might not get what I'm looking for. Do you want me to help you gather the books or should I wait until you give a signal?" His laugh turned into a grin. If his current actions were anything to go by this man wouldn't be easy to deal with., she could see herself falling for that smile.

"Are you okay, Ms. Mason?" Said Sweet Bloom's oldest security guard as he walked unsteadily towards them.

"I'm good, Charles," Lydia said. Could this situation get any worse? Sweet Blooms was a small town, and that meant news traveled faster than electricity through walls. The news would probably beat her home that she had literally run into Ethan. From there she could expect a love child any week. Charles Lyndman had been the security guard at the courthouse since she had left to go to law school. The town knew he was too old to find anything else, so he kept the job of guarding the one place where there was nothing of value. She knew as soon as he went inside, he'd call four of his friends about the excitement on the steps.

"I saw you coming up the steps, but you looked like you had it," he mumbled.

"At least someone had clear sight," Lydia said, staring at Ethan.

Tapping his glasses, he smiled. "I've had my sight checked, and I'm sure it's good."

"Keep it up, and I'll have the security guard arrest you."

Ethan's grin got wider. He looked over her shoulder at the rotund elderly guard. "If he did, it looks like it would be a first for any of that equipment. I'm not here to cause a problem I just wanted to speak with you. Let me try to make this right."

"Make it right?" Lydia parroted.

Ethan bent and began to gather the books, handing one or two over to the security guard before sending him on his way to the table inside the doors. "After all, I'd feel bad if I didn't finish helping you."

Just as she was going to refute that he had even helped at all, a gust of wind came by and blew several papers down the steps. Lydia flew down two steps and leaped onto the fleeing paper to stop it. She heard him clapping behind her, and Lydia closed her eyes. She just needed to gather her papers and send him on his way.

Lydia Mason was who she was, and she wasn't going to get her head turned around by an attractive man. She was the Mayor's daughter who had to be beyond reproach all the time. She was a lawyer, and hopefully the town would recognize her as being one instead of just Mayor Mason's kid who happened to get a law degree. She had proven she was self-sufficient when she paid for law school on her own. Well, not completely because she had school loan debt, but anything loans didn't cover, she did.

"Ms. Mason?"

"Yes?" she said sharply.

Ethan was kneeling down before her with his hand on the small batch of papers she had stopped with her foot. Lydia had to admit there was something thrilling having Ethan kneeling in front of her. It was almost romantic in a Cinderella kind of way. "Ms. Mason, did you want me to put the papers back in order? If you do, you'll have to move your foot."

While she was in la-la land, he was waiting for an answer. She picked up her foot and nodded.

"That's what I like to see, us working together,"

Ethan said with a grin. She looked around, trying to collect herself. Then she heard his voice again seeping into her thoughts. "How about dinner tonight?"

Dinner? she thought. *Great, it sounded like he was staying in town.* She needed to nip this in the bud.

"Sure, where?"

"I'll come get you. It'll be a surprise."

Lydia hated surprises. She didn't get a chance to respond because Ethan had already walked away. She was so concentrated on him; she didn't even notice the security guard had come out several times to finish moving the books.

"That was mighty nice of him to help you out," Mr. Lyndman said.

A nice smile and an easy demeanor were slow to slip past the defenses, she thought. Harmlessness wrapped up with a pair of glasses. Ethan Young was a lot of things, but she wouldn't have attributed harmlessness to him. When she'd been in his arms for a moment, she'd forgotten that he wanted something from her. For a moment, she'd had an experience that might have been something more.

She couldn't say it was intimate, but she could say it was something she hadn't experienced lately. In Sweet Blooms, she had to think about people who approached her. She was never sure if they were saying hello to Lydia Mason or the Mayor's daughter.

If nothing else, she was sure that Ethan was definitely not interested in Lydia Mason.

Ethan Young knew a lot of things. In fact, knowing things was his business. The new bit of information he had just acquired was that he was definitely interested in Lydia Mason. He had to get his head in the game of real estate and out of beautiful blondes on courthouse steps.

Ethan had arranged a meeting with his business associate, Adam Cade. He'd worked for many days doing the research he thought would be needed to get Cade's support. He knew Cade wasn't a man who invested based on sentimentality, yet he was still going to try to invoke some of that in this presentation.

It was funny to him that he was in a spare room in the courthouse, waiting for Cade. There weren't any places to rent office space and if you wanted to have a business meeting in Sweet Blooms, but didn't have your own building, the only option was to rent a room from the courthouse. Ethan thought the room looked suspiciously like a holding cell, or an interrogation room, but beggars couldn't be choosy.

The gray walls didn't do anything to inspire him, nor did the single window that looked like a last-minute placement. However, Ethan thought he should probably be grateful the rectangular table was at least clean, and while the two chairs in the room were hard, they were relatively new.

Funny how time changed things. Ethan was back. He had never lost track of his hometown. It was because he was watching it that he was able to spot an answer to the town's potential problem. Sweet Blooms would collapse under the debt it was starting to accumulate. He had seen other towns go down this road. They hadn't been able to collect the taxes, and it started a vicious cycle of people leaving the town. Ethan didn't like Sweet Blooms all of the time, but it was still home.

Ethan thought he would be able to leave Sweet Blooms behind. When he thought about the last time he had been in Sweet Blooms, though, he reconsidered. When he thought about all of the returned envelopes he received from his father, he considered abandoning Sweet Blooms. The only thing that had made him give the town a second chance was when he thought about all of the good times he had with his dad.

How many times had they gone fishing. How his dad taught him to know when a storm was coming, or how his dad had taught him to smell the coming rain. Some other child would never know that or have those experiences if Sweet Blooms went away. It was after remembering those things that he swallowed any protests he might have and had and came up with a solution.

Ethan had done his research and discovered that Adam Cade was also from Sweet Blooms. As soon as he had identified the millionaire woodworker as a Sweet Blooms native, he started formulating a plan to save Sweet Blooms. Whether they wanted him or not, Ethan was going to save Sweet Blooms.

Ethan had set up the room with a projector, two paper printouts of the Power Point presentation, and a laptop. Ethan heard a knock, and then Adam Cade walked in. They shook hands, and Adam took the seat that gave him the best view of the screen. Ethan smiled and sat in the other chair to begin.

"Make yourself at home," Ethan said. "It's odd that we're both back here, but I think after the presentation, it will be clear to you why I asked you."

Adam nodded, and Ethan began the presentation.

"Sweet Blooms is in trouble. Over the past ten years, while all of Florida has experienced an insurgence and growth due to retirees and snowbirds, Sweet Blooms hasn't fared as well. In fact, it's like the town that time forgot. With the birthrate being low and no new income from new people, it becomes almost impossible for Sweet Blooms to maintain much less thrive.

"After reviewing Sweet Blooms' assets, I've found it only has two things: nostalgic stores and land. If we can convert the land into more stores owned by locals, and expand, we can bring people here to visit.

"All of this is possible in time, but Sweet Blooms doesn't have a lot of that. That's why I called you. You own Cade Designs, and you're a Sweet Blooms native. If you could do an ad campaign or put a store here with your designs, it would give Sweet Blooms time and a boost all at once. If you don't, you should know that several real estate companies have been looking at Sweet Blooms to find the best way to take over the land with minimal effort."

Adam tapped the table rhythmically. "I did some looking before I came. Almost all of the land in Sweet Blooms is owned by a real estate holding called Outskirts, Inc."

"It is."

Ethan continued with several other slides, showing the potential growth of Sweet Blooms and what kind of businesses could be fostered. He outlined a couple of ideas he had and looked at Adam the whole time. When he was outlining the earning potential and how Cade Designs could recoup its money, he turned off the computer.

Adam gave him a long look. "You're Barrack's son?"

Ethan stiffened and then nodded, forcing himself to relax.

Adam nodded towards the screen. "You did a great job with the presentation. Are you representing an agency?"

"No, the idea is mine."

Adam gave him a second look.

Ethan gave him a smile. "I know what you're thinking. Why would a person from the outskirts care to do this?"

Adam shook his head. "No, I didn't think that at all," he said with a smile.

Ethan stopped talking and waited.

"I know there have always been people who have issues with those who live on the outskirts. I'm not one of them. I asked if the idea was yours or not because you don't live in Sweet Blooms. Are you coming back? Will you be keeping the real estate yourself?"

Ethan was taken aback by the question. He shouldn't have been. For the last ten years, he'd been making money from making deals. He was sure that Adam knew of him even though they had never worked together.

Adam didn't wait for an answer. "I think you've done a lot of research and you make a compelling argument. I'm currently trying to figure out some things that may fall in line with this. I want to tell you that you've done well by the people in Sweet Blooms today, Ethan Young. Send me some paperwork so I can go over it with my marketing team and lawyers."

Ethan nodded. "Of course." Ethan didn't say anything when Adam got up to leave the room. The door opened, and Adam cleared his throat.

"By the way, Ethan, I asked to let my lawyers see it not because of who you are but because this is about Sweet Blooms. Business is business."

Adam left, and Ethan smiled. Until Adam said it out loud, he had wondered. If Cade could get past him being from the outskirts, he could too.

Two

Lydia had received a text saying to be ready by four. She was already prepping herself to tell him how she didn't like to be dictated to. If he wanted to have a partnership, he had to at least pretend it was one. When the car appeared outside of her house instead of him, she gave a second look to her attire. She had decided to put on a simple blue sundress with a white cardigan and matching blue and white shoes. It was too late to go back, so she left and got into the car. The ride wasn't long, but she could tell she was being taken into a nearby county. When the car stopped, the door was opened, and she could see that she was in front of a well-known restaurant that she had only heard of: Carter's.

When she walked into the restaurant, she expected him to be there, but he wasn't. Instead, the maitre'd showed her to the table that had been reserved for her. After sitting there for ten minutes, she thought she would leave and curse Ethan Young later. Just as it was set in her mind to do so, she saw him walking towards her.

She admitted he could carry off corporate casual well. He had on blue trousers and a blue pinstriped shirt. It was topped off with a blue blazer and enough attitude to make anyone take notice.

He took a seat across from her. Lydia looked at her watch. "Are you sure you gave me the right time?" she asked.

Ethan sighed and shook his head. "I wouldn't blame you for being upset."

Lydia looked around the dimly lit restaurant. She knew it was supposed to be romantic. The sconces on the wall, the tables separated with just enough distance to give privacy. The floor was carpeted with a maroon color. When customers and waiters walked the floors, the footfalls were cushioned so as not to disturb the other diners.

"Are you ready to order?" he asked with an easy smile.

"I was ready fifteen minutes ago, now the urge to eat has passed."

She watched him stop for a minute, and she could have sworn she saw a look of frustration pass across his visage. Then he surprised her.

"If you're not ready to eat, we can leave and do desserts if you want."

She gave him a second look and then reached out to pick up a menu.

"You're not what I thought you'd be, Ethan Young."

His smile turned into a grin and the laughter filtered into his eyes. "I try to keep people guessing."

When the waiter came to the table, Ethan turned towards him and ordered drinks. When he motioned to her menu, she nodded for him to go on.

Ethan ordered from the menu and settled back in his chair once the waiter left.

"You order as if you know the menu. Do you come here a lot?" she asked.

Ethan smiled. "I feel like I'll be judged no matter how I answer this."

"Really?"

"If I say I bring business associates here, you'll think this is business. If I say I bring others, you'll think I meant to wine and dine you."

"Well which one is it? Why did you bring me here?"

The waiter returned and brought the drinks and appetizers.

"I brought you here because I wanted to talk to another fellow resident of Sweet Blooms," he said.

Lydia tapped her foot on the floor, watching Ethan take a sip from his glass.

"Is this when you tell me you've been to Sweet Blooms and you were so taken with it that you wanted to move here?"

Ethan smiled and shook his head. "No, I didn't discover Sweet Blooms. I was born here."

She stopped and gave him a hard look. "I know all of the important families here."

"Ouch! My father is Barrick Young."

Lydia groaned and pretended to be extremely interested in her appetizer. The main course wasn't even here, and she had already called him a liar and offended him. Fortunately, a few minutes later the waiter came and cleared the table and brought the entrees. The conversation was kept to the meal and the weather. When the food was taken away, Ethan broke the silence.

"I didn't know the announcement would be such a shocker. I assure you there's nothing you could say that would offend me, and now you know why."

Lydia knew Barrick Young was on the outskirts. "Is that why you're here? Because of your family?"

"Maybe a bit of it. I do think it's a bit ironic that one of the people the town would think twice about entertaining would be one of the people who would want to help them."

Lydia nodded and took a deep breath. "It's true, that will give some people pause."

He grinned. "I didn't plan on saying the son of Barrick Young wants to save Sweet Blooms."

"It would be nice if you had others on your side."

Ethan agreed. "I had that same thought and reached out to Adam Cade. He'll be joining me."

Her mouth fell open. "He's come to help when the town needs it, but this is way more."

Ethan launched. "I know, and he's a great businessman. I think I was able to put together a plan that would work for him."

Lydia rolled the stem of her wine glass between her fingers. "Tell me about yourself, Ethan Young. What have you been doing since your departure from Sweet Blooms?"

"I've been doing real estate since I left. I will say the one thing my dad was really big about was a man needing to own the land that he lives on. As a result, he taught me all he knew about looking at land and how to evaluate it. I took that, went to large developers, and helped them to find land that they could build on. It turned out that what my dad knows is pretty valuable amongst the city realtors, and I made a good, decent living with it."

"Well, Sweet Blooms will have to take some time and re-evaluate its natural resources."

His slow grin came back with an ease that said the evening had changed from townies meeting to something far more intimate.

"Is that what you're doing tonight? Taking inventory of natural resources."

Lydia considered his question and ignored it. "So, you decided to come back to Sweet Blooms after you acquired some fortune?"

Ethan chuckled. "The way you say it makes it sound like after I made my fortune, I came home. I like to think my home needed me, and I just so happen to have money as well."

Lydia focused on the ease with which Ethan handled himself and thought about what she knew of Barrick Young. This man had been shaped and molded in a different world. He might have started in Sweet Blooms, but she didn't know how much he really remembered about small towns.

"Do you plan on being here the whole time while Sweet Blooms gets on its feet? Or are you only here until a decision is made one way or another on what to do in Sweet Blooms?"

"I'll stay to see it through and make my decisions then."

Lydia looked at him as he spoke. "I'm not sure that everyone will be comfortable with you being on the site," she said. "You know your father can be a little rough to be around, and you have to figure that's going to play into how people interact with you."

"I was hoping things had changed."

Lydia snorted. "Sweet Blooms has its good, its bad, and its ugly just like any other place."

"So, you don't think the people of Sweet Blooms can get past their prejudice?"

"I think I expect people to be people."

"It's funny you say that. You know I'm not my father. I didn't even have to meet with you at all. I could have waited a couple of months and brought some developers here and moved everyone off the land except for the people in the outskirts."

Lydia had locked gazes with him as he spoke. At that moment there were the two competing emotions of interest and intent. She had never met him before, but she knew he wasn't the boy he had been. Now he was life hardened and a man who made his own path. She was aware of him on several levels, and rivalry wasn't the only one.

Of course, it would figure that she would like the man who had come to either save or destroy Sweet Blooms.

"You've already talked Cade into saving us."

Ethan smiled. "I've already talked to Adam Cade about coming to Sweet Blooms and setting up. I haven't discussed who will own Sweet Blooms' land or, better yet, who owns it now."

Lydia looked at Ethan and tried to understand what was going on.

"What are you saying, Ethan? Just say it and be done."

"I'm saying I will save Sweet Blooms."

"Who will save it from you?"

"You don't need to worry. I'm a native."

Lydia put her napkin on the table. "I don't think it works that way at all. I think this kind of loophole you have, of you owning the town, speaks to your character. Perhaps that isn't the kind of person we want to own Sweet Blooms. You could gift the land back; that is if you own it."

All of the charm left his face, and Lydia was sure she was looking at the face of the man who had made a fortune in real estate. "You don't want my kind owning Sweet Blooms?"

"I think your kind will be determined when you do the right thing and give the land back to the town."

Lydia realized she had made a mistake not taking his calls earlier. If she had just taken the call, then he wouldn't be here in the flesh. Ethan Young in the flesh couldn't be ignored or put off.

Ethan leaned on the table. "You don't find it a bit self-serving that the only way I can be seen as decent is to do whatever it is you want me to do?"

"In this case, self-serving and the right thing are the same thing."

When he didn't respond, Lydia stood up. "I think it's time I left."

Ethan stood at the same time. Lydia put out her hand. "I can get myself home."

Ethan motioned towards the door. When they went by the maitre'd, he told her to put the meal on his tab. When they were finally outside, the car was waiting for Lydia.

"Contrary to what you may think about my kind, I do know how to treat a lady. I brought you here. I'll deliver you back. And don't worry, I have no intentions of imposing my presence upon you. I thought we would be celebrating saving Sweet Blooms. Obviously, who saves it and how is more important than the final act."

With that, Ethan walked away and got into another car. Lydia called herself all kinds of fool on the way home. She and Sweet Blooms had to step out of the past and into the future if they wanted to survive.

Lydia Mason was the special counsel to the Mayor. In Sweet Blooms, it was said that she was either special because she was the only counsel in Sweet Blooms, or special because she was the Mayor's daughter.

Before going into work, she ran five miles. Today, recalling her bad behavior at dinner plagued all five of those miles. She worked all morning at refocusing her thoughts for the day. By the time she walked into the office, she was prepared for the mounds of paperwork that had to be reviewed and filed, and for the motions to be put in for the judge that came to Sweet Blooms three times a week. She remembered that the reason she herself left Sweet Blooms in the first place was to become more than the Mayor's daughter. To leave the small minds and pettiness of Sweet Blooms.

Today she couldn't focus on a single paper because she felt so guilty for having fallen into the same category she had run away from. She had been way out of line. She blamed it on a combination of things. It was the shock of hearing how close Sweet Blooms was to being in default. It was the fact that she thought she had been the one in control, yet it turned out Ethan Young held all the cards. It was her sense of helplessness that made her strike out at a man who frightened her with the calmness of how he spoke about taking the town she lived in.

Even as she took her seat behind her desk and opened the first folder on the stack to be done, she knew she would have to deal with Ethan. She had prejudged him and potentially misjudged him based on nothing else but where he had lived. She wondered if she was so quick to see the negative in him because he was the first man in a long time who had managed to catch her attention long enough for her to actually see that all men were not created equally. Ethan had been given his fair share and then some.

As if her thoughts conjured him, she looked up to see Ethan Young standing at her door. She didn't even want to think about how long he'd been standing there, or how deep in thought she had to have been to not hear him coming down the wooden hallway.

She took a quick gander around her office and stuck her chin up higher. She knew what he would see. A large desk set in a room that was too small to really hold it. Four walls decorated with all of the Mayor's achievements. It was a testament to the fact that this room used to be the Mayor's achievement room. There were only two windows in the office. One of them was blocked by a portable air conditioner that rattled as if it were on its last days. The other window could use a cleaning.

Despite her surroundings, she focused on him, trying to find a way to make amends with a man who was way out of her league. In the daylight, unencumbered by books or angling up steps, she could see his suits were tailored to his shape. When his hand was in his pocket, it didn't break any lines in the open jacket he wore. The words that came to mind were *handsome professor*. She could see the hint of shape from his toned legs and muscled arms beneath his tailored clothing—just enough to know without doubt he was well built.

This was a man who could wear anything and still stand out in a crowd. It wasn't what he wore. It wasn't what he owned. It was Ethan Young. It was that something that couldn't be defined that was an intricate part of him. It was the thing that made her notice him and the same thing that made her cautious.

She'd made assumptions about Ethan. When he walked into the office, he sat in the only other chair in the room and dropped a folded document on her desk. She hoped Sweet Blooms wasn't going to pay for her mistakes.

She'd prided herself on being fair, on giving everyone a chance, but with this man she had forgotten that. She reached out and unfolded the document.

"You can file that in the courthouse," he said.

"What is it?" she asked as she skimmed the document, hoping she was reading it wrong.

Ethan smiled. "Counsel, it's proof that I own 75% of Sweet Blooms. You shop owners have always let the town manage their lots. The town, in turn, put them up as collateral against increasing debt. I bought it and thereby bought 75% of Sweet Blooms."

She put the paper down.

"I was wrong. Is that what you want me to say? I passed judgment on you based on your past. I don't usually do that, but you make me antsy."

"I hope you don't take this approach in court. If so, I can't see you being very good in persuading people to go your way."

Lydia gritted her teeth. "I don't usually have to persuade anyone. I'm usually right."

He tapped the table. "I still think lawyers should know how to negotiate," he said with a smile.

Lydia leaned forward and looked him square in the eye. "Fine, let's negotiate."

Ethan chuckled. "I would, but you don't have anything to put on the table."

"I can do something for you, Ethan, that your money can't buy," she whispered.

"This I have to hear."

Lydia sat back and held up her hand. "You have to hear the whole deal first."

Ethan nodded in agreement.

"If you give me the time it takes you to set up things in Sweet Blooms, I'll show you a town that you should give the land back to." Lydia threw out the bait and waited to see if Ethan would take it. Lydia remembered the stories about Barrick and how they were treated. She couldn't imagine a positive outcome with the tables turned.

Ethan laughed. "Unless you can go back in time, I don't think you can do that."

"What I can do is wipe your slate clean."

"Really? And how would you do that, assuming that's what I want?"

"Here's my thought. No one would recognize you now. If we tell everyone who you are, they would treat you differently, probably out of fear." Lydia took a deep breath and attempted to steady herself. "I'm suggesting that you pose as my boyfriend."

Ethan's mouth immediately quirked up at the side and his eyes positively twinkled at the strange proposition.

She tried to stamp down her suddenly hammering heart and fluttering stomach and quickly went on, "Doing so would enable you to get a clean slate and a different view of Sweet Blooms, which would help you realize not everyone is narrow-minded. There are some great things and people in Sweet Blooms that make them trustworthy enough to own their own town."

"Your townsfolk lost Sweet Blooms because they can't handle money."

"You can still control that and give the land rights to the town. I'm asking for a chance to show you a different side of Sweet Blooms."

"Do you think I'm so desperate to be accepted by Sweet Blooms that I'll say yes to this?"

Lydia shook her head. "I think I'm the desperate one wanting to save her home."

"And you think I'll ruin it?" he asked tightly.

Lydia smiled. "I think you need to know what it's really like. I think you've only seen the worst. I assume that people make the worst assumptions about you, like I did."

"They do."

"It won't happen if you do this my way. It's not forever, either. It's until things get set up."

Ethan grinned. "You think you can rehabilitate me into a better, more human person?"

"Not a chance. I think you're fair, and you're less judgmental than I was."

Ethan stood up and went to the door. He turned and gave her an intense look that made her want to squirm.

"Lydia Mason, I was wrong. You do know how to negotiate." He towards her and winked, "I accept."

Lydia waited until she heard the door at the end of

the hall close before she let out a big breath. She got up and, for once, closed her door and went to stand in front of the air conditioner. She was attracted to the man who held the fate of Sweet Blooms in his hands.

Her law profession had once told her that when the defense and the prosecutor seemed to like each other, it made for a stimulating case and was called a sweet attraction.

This was one sweet attraction she could have done without.

Three

Ethan had decided to take Lydia up on her offer. He had to admit him making that decision had everything to do with Lydia and nothing to do with business. Ethan had known beautiful women, but Lydia had that something else about her. When she talked about Sweet Blooms, he could hear her passion and love for her home. He could also see the way she was trying to maneuver him, even though he held all the cards. He admired her boldness and crusader spirit.

Ethan was never one to avoid issues. Now that he had met Lydia it was time to face his dad. He rented a truck and drove home. No matter how many business deals he had prepped for, there was nothing in his repertoire that he could call on to help him with this meeting. It would be seventeen years of separation.

Too soon he was in front of the house where he saw his dad standing on the front porch. He didn't dawdle in the truck; he got out and went to the bottom step of the porch.

"You lost?" Barrick Young started.

Ethan almost stepped back. Did he look so different? He warred with indecision and hurt.

"You heard me, Ethan. Are you lost?"

Ethan let out a sigh of relief. "Why would you even say that?"

"I figure that could be the only reason you're back here."

"You've gotten a little grey and have a little paunch," Ethan said, pointing at his dad's middle.

"You've gotten older and obviously have forgotten how to go get your own switch so your elders can show you what happens to disrespectful children," Barrick grumbled back.

"You've never sent me to get a switch," he countered.

Barrick shrugged, "Maybe you're slower in your old age."

Ethan took a step onto the porch. "I wanted to talk to you."

"I haven't moved."

"You haven't answered any of my letters. You sent all of them back."

Barrick shrugged. "If it was important, you'd come and tell me."

"I'm home."

Barrick looked at him for a moment, nodded, and went to sit on one of the two chairs on the porch. Ethan took that as an invitation and went to sit on the other chair. He didn't pay attention to how the porch needed to be scraped and painted. Or how the house was a little shabbier than when he had left it.

"Why are you home, Ethan?"

Ethan stopped rocking the chair. "I came home to help Sweet Blooms."

Barrick looked at Ethan and then rocked back and laughed.

"It's true!"

"You've been away awhile. You're telling yourself stories just like city folk do."

Evan stopped rocking and looked at his father. "I don't get it."

Barrick looked at him and nodded. "I think you're here for a lot of reasons, Ethan, but none of them are for Sweet Blooms. I only have to look at your stock to tell you. Neither I, nor your mother, ever did anything for anyone but ourselves. It doesn't have to be pretty, but it's true. I'd be really surprised if you broke that mold."

"I've got money."

"True."

"I've got property."

Barrick looked over at his son. "Then it seems you've come to Sweet Blooms to get something money can't buy."

"Why is it always this way with you? Black or white. Go or no go. There's never a gray."

Barrick stood up and shook his head. "The problem isn't about me and gray. It's about you thinking that if you have money and things, it'll change who you are. It won't. I'll be seeing you in town, I suppose, that is if you can be seen with me."

With that, Barrick went in and Ethan just leaned his head back on the rocking chair. He didn't know how long he sat out there, but it was long enough for the sun to go down. Then he stood up slowly and went to the hotel.

Ethan got into his truck and realized he had nowhere to go. He had thought things would go a lot of different ways, but this wasn't one of them.

If Ethan was honest with himself, he realized that he thought Sweet Blooms would welcome him as a hero, and he thought his father would come out and be proud of what he'd already done.

He had a fortune, he would have considered himself an educated man, and he'd put the money into Sweet Blooms to give him a right to be here. He'd go to Lydia Mason. If he treated this like any other deal, he'd be successful. Meeting his dad had thrown him, but there was still time to see this go right.

"Pull it together, Ethan," he warned, trying to shake the frustration that was building up. He started the truck and went to the beginning of it all.

The drive from the hotel to the courthouse was short. When he pulled into the parking lot, there were several cars and trucks there. He couldn't imagine what had happened in Sweet Blooms that all of these people needed a lawyer. When he walked into the courthouse, it was clear. In front of the security check-in was a sign that said Free Legal Help Today. When he was through the check-in and followed the sign around the corner, he walked into a long line of what looked like poor townsfolk and citizens from the outskirts of town. As he walked by the line that snaked down the hall and into an office around the corner, he found Lydia and another woman in the room.

This office was different than the one he saw her in yesterday. It was large enough for the two desks, and there was just enough space that they could have some privacy. As if on cue, Lydia lifted her head and mouthed for him to wait.

Ethan left the office and noticed the small table next to the door. It had a signup sheet. On the sheet, he saw the name of the person and the reason they were here in the second column. People were there for wills, property disputes, separations, alimony, and worker's compensation. In the next two columns were the names Lydia Mason and Yolanda Street.

When he peeked in the room again, he saw Lydia intently listening to the woman in the chair. The woman was obviously from the outskirts. Her clothes were handmade, and the baby she was bouncing on her knee was focused on pulling the papers off the desk. As the woman spoke, he saw Lydia move the items out of the way without breaking stride. Ethan watched Lydia reach out to calm the woman. He realized that's what he wanted. He wanted to come to make a difference.

Lydia finished quicker than he would have expected. She stood up from the desk and nodded politely to her friend and tapped Ethan on the shoulder as she walked out of the room.

They went down a hall, and neither one of them spoke. When she pushed open the door, they were in a reception area. There was a large desk with an older woman sitting at it. The nameplate read Amanda Ollier, secretary to the mayor.

Lydia held up her hand. "Stay here. I need to get my jacket and make a stop at the bathroom." He nodded, and she went through a side door.

Then he heard the secretary clear her throat.

"You're Ethan Young," she said, smiling and extending her hand out for him to shake. "I'm Amanda Ollier, as my plate says, secretary to the mayor and the file clerk for the courthouse."

Understanding dawned on Ethan. Some things

never changed in Sweet Blooms. Somehow, he had managed not to notice the titled secretary to the mayor. He smiled and gave his attention to her. "I'm glad to make your acquaintance."

He shook her hand and waited.

Amanda was in her late thirties, with auburn hair and eyes that looked artificially blue. He could tell she was about average height, and if today's outfit was any indication, he would say she wore white blouses, dark skirts, and matching black shoes daily.

"I saw that you own quite a bit of Sweet Blooms," Amanda said.

"I'm into realty. Sweet Blooms is a sound investment."

"Well, let me know if you need anyone to show you around."

Ethan smiled. "Thank you."

When he said thank you, her smile grew a little wider. "It can be lonely being a newcomer in a small town."

Ethan nodded. It was funny how time could change how people looked at you. He could tell she thought this was going well.

"For you to afford all of that property, you must make a lot of money doing your job," she said.

Okay, it wasn't subtle, but this was Sweet Blooms.

Lydia had her hand on the door and had pushed it just enough to crack it and hear the conversation going on between Ethan and Amanda. She heard him going along with Amanda as if he were a new person in Sweet Blooms. She wasn't looking at him, but his tone was so bland she was surprised that Amanda couldn't hear his disinterest. This conversation was a bit too close to his impression of everybody. This conversation would only confirm his worst thoughts about the town. That the people of Sweet Blooms were a bit shallow and needed titles more than they cared about individuals.

Lydia pushed the door open and walked over to Ethan.

"I can see the two of you have met. I told Ethan it wouldn't take long for people to know he was here."

Ethan just smiled and didn't say a word. When she looped her arm through his, she felt him tense up, but he didn't pull away from her.

Amanda looked pointedly at their interlocked arms. "I didn't know you knew Ethan," she said, looking at Lydia. Then the phone rang.

"Excuse me," Amanda said as she answered the phone.

"Of course." Lydia waited until she knew Amanda would be on the phone for a moment and then walked Ethan toward the door. When they were outside, she had to ask him, "So why didn't you tell Amanda that you're a native?"

Ethan shrugged. "I gave your proposition some thought."

"You mean you think there's some good in Sweet Blooms?" she asked.

"No, I haven't bought into that, but I'm willing to let you try so you can see people are people. Having me keep the rights to the town won't make a difference either way."

"You're being so magnanimous."

"I can afford to be generous. I'm going to win."

Lydia snorted. As they walked into the parking lot, she stopped them. "Let's go for a walk?"

Lydia loved the town of Sweet Blooms. It had that country flair that looked like it came straight from a picture book. The sidewalks were made of red brick, not poured squared cement blocks. Every eighteen inches there was a metal post with a ring in it. They had all been painted a bright color to match the flowers that bloomed in the area. The posts were throwbacks to the days when there were horses in Sweet Blooms. With cobbled streets and a total of four traffic lights in the whole town, Lydia always thought Sweet Blooms was the perfect town to model a gingerbread town after.

They had walked for three blocks and gone by several stores when she saw some chairs on the sidewalk outside of the juice bar. The juice bar had opened up within the last six months.

"You like this juice bar?" Ethan asked.

Lydia smiled. "Yes. The name I would redo. I mean, who names a juice bar The Squeeze?"

Ethan laughed. "I do."

Lydia stopped laughing and looked at him.

"Seriously?"

Ethan nodded. "So, if we're going to pull off this idea that we're together, I think I need to know some things."

Lydia gave him a long look before she answered. "You ask, and I'll see if it's really any of your business to know the answer."

A waitress came out, and before she could rattle off the day's drinks, Ethan answered. "Can we have a number four and a number six?"

The high school student nodded, bobbing her ponytail. When she left, Lydia looked at him. "How did you know?"

Ethan smiled. "How did I know that you usually order number four or that I would like number six?"

"Both."

"The first is easy. I watch all of my investments, and this one is no different. I've been to Sweet Blooms many times, and I've seen you. When I'm here, I have the number six."

Lydia looked at him for a moment. "Don't you think that's kind of creepy?"

Ethan laughed. "I never think watching my money is creepy, and if that's your thought, I can understand why Sweet Blooms is in the predicament it's in now."

Lydia waved him off. "Ask your questions."

"Why don't you have a man in your life?"

"Because I'm a pain to deal with, according to my last relationship."

"Really?"

Lydia smiled. "Yes, he insisted that I was bossy. I was goal orientated and didn't have the right balance of ambition and womanliness to keep a man happy."

Ethan smirked. "It sounds like you two had some interesting times. Should I be nervous?"

Lydia looked him over. "Only if you're easily intimidated by women who think."

Ethan grinned. "Then I have nothing to worry about at all, as I prefer my women to have a mind of their own."

"So, they all say."

The waitress came by and delivered the smoothies. After taking a few deep sips, she broke the silence.

"You know, when Amanda brought up how much of Sweet Blooms you had bought, you could have said no to everything then," she began.

"I could have, but I had visited my dad last night. I told him I was back."

Lydia whistled. "That must have been some kind of family reunion. I don't know the relationship the two of you have, but I would think he'd be happy with your success. At the very least that he'd be happy with you saving the town."

Ethan took another sip of his juice and looked into the plastic container.

"He listened to what I had to say. He was more interested in what my motivation was to come back and less about my money."

Lydia exhaled. "That sounds like something my mother would ask."

Ethan looked at her. "So, what are you saying, that all parents are the same and working from the same handbook?"

"Never say that's true," Lydia said through her laughter after placing her hand on her chest in mock horror. "But I think they are definitely sharing the same school of thought."

"Listen, I expect people to see my money way before they see me. Sometimes my money changes history, and they remember me differently."

"Differently?"

Ethan nodded. "You'd be amazed how quick people will be to blame my past behavior on anything and anyone else so they can say they always saw the good in me."

Lydia studied him and gave a sad smile. "I'm sorry I fell into that group."

Ethan lightly wrapped the tabletop and Lydia looked up. "Don't be sad. I understand people, and I've been around enough to know when people are sincere. I appreciate your apology."

"Thanks for being so understanding."

Ethan smiled. "I have to say, whenever I get an apology from a beautiful woman, the issue is all but forgotten."

Lydia raised her eyebrows. "Really?"

Ethan shrugged. "Within reason, yes."

Taking him up on the offer, she smiled and leaned forward. "Well, if that's the case, let's go back to our original agreement. I'll show you a different side of the world if you let me. I'll give you a new beginning while we discover the good in the people of Sweet Blooms."

Ethan stared at her and then tilted his head to the side. Lydia was about to start fidgeting under his gaze when he spoke.

"I find myself in an odd place, Lydia. I know what has always been and what I think will always be. But when I hear you talk, you seem so convinced, that I have to think there must be something you see that I don't. So, the short answer is yes, we have a deal. During the time it takes for me to get everything together to save Sweet Blooms, you can show me their stellar character."

Lydia wasn't thrilled with his sarcasm and needed to even things out.

"It's quid pro quo. Why aren't you with someone?"

Ethan laughed. "If you believe what my last relationship said, the reason I don't have a steady relationship is because I'm already in one with my career. She said no woman would play second fiddle to the hours I worked."

"Was she right?"

Ethan stared at her again and then looked at his drink. "It's funny. When I first get into a relationship, I think I've vetted the woman so well. I make sure that she's all career-minded and focused. In the beginning, they all said yes, but in the end, they all changed their tunes. I can be focused on work. I don't deny that, but I think we all need to be honest about what we will and won't do."

How odd it was to hear this conversation. This had been the conversation with her last love interest. He had accused her of being too focused, and she had accused him of not understanding she was goal driven. Lydia had always felt as though he was trying to make her choose between him and her career.

They may have been born on the opposite parts of town, but they shared the same problems when it came to relationships.

Four

Lydia braced herself for the late lunch. She thought today was going to be a win. The free clinic was going great. She had gotten Ethan on board to give Sweet Blooms a chance and then it went downhill. Her mother hadn't called her on her personal phone. Instead, the secretary of the Mayor called and set up an appointment for them.

The Banter House was Lydia's go-to place to get lunch. The Banter House was a renovated bar turned diner and it had all of the wood paneling and the new booths installed in the main dining room. The waitresses were mostly the girls from the local high school during the day and from the community college in the evening.

The most important thing about The Banter House was that Mayor Mason hated it. Lydia could admit it was a petty thing to book the lunch here, but it was the only way to respond to having your mother's secretary set up lunch.

Lydia watched her mother walk into the Banter House and scan the room for her. Of course, her mother was dressed in a linen cream suit. Lydia had no idea how her mother kept that suit clean. She knew her mother preferred light colors and never sported a stain. Ever. She, on the other hand, had on a black skirt with a red blouse. The blouse had a dark stain on it from the bacon grease that dripped from her breakfast sandwich.

"Hello, Mayor," Lydia said to her mother. "I wasn't sure what the meeting was about, so I picked a place I'd be comfortable." She looked around and nodded.

"I'm sure you did what you thought was best."

Lydia knew her mother never thought she did what was best. Lydia couldn't tell when their relationship had gone south, she could only say that they had lost each other along the way.

"What can I do for you?"

Mara Mason might have been the epitome of calm and stability to everyone else, but right now she was a fidgety woman who ran her hand over her sleeve ever so often as if to remind herself where she was and who she was with.

"I'm here because I've looked at the papers and Amanda told me who you were with. I thought it was time for me to meet Ethan Young."

Lydia laughed. "I suppose it is. What is it? Are you concerned that I might not represent you correctly?"

Mara stopped and stared at Lydia. "You have a habit of being a bit aggressive. I thought I could talk to him and then we could come to some agreement."

"You do know I'm a lawyer, right?"

"You do know I'm your mother, right?"

Lydia leaned back. "I'm sorry. I didn't mean to sound that way. I'm just saying that I went to school to learn how to negotiate and—"

"And in less than five minutes with me, you've already lost your edge, and had it been with anyone else, you would have given more ground to the other side because of your uncontrolled passion."

Lydia sat back and looked at her mother. "You've always told me to follow my dreams. You told me nothing was out of my reach. When I reach for it, then you say I have too much uncontrolled passion."

Mara reached out across the table and held her hand up, waiting for Lydia's. "Yes, I said you can have anything. But you don't want anything. You want everything."

When Lydia didn't put her hand in her mother's, Mara drew it back. In a matter of seconds, any softness she had seen before was gone. Lydia was about to say something, but when she looked across the table, the moment was gone and in her mother's, face was replaced by the Mayor of Sweet Blooms.

"What is the relationship between you and Ethan?"

Lydia gasped when she heard the words. "The relationship? When you say it, it's full of implied innuendo."

"There's nothing implied when a man comes to town and then spends the first three days seeing one woman. You go out with him for lunch, and you're seen filing his deeds and leases as if he is a private client. When it's all said and done, the question really is, is Ethan business or pleasure?"

"No," Lydia snapped back. "It's not personal like you think. I don't have some delusion that I'm falling in love. This isn't what you think. He wanted some help. I'm advising him on what he should do and what is in the best interest of Sweet Blooms. It is true that

I'm helping him, but it's because I like to help people. Just count it towards one of my unconditional passions."

The Mayor leaned back in the booth and harrumphed. A waitress came by to the table. Without taking her eyes off of Lydia, Mayor Mason waved the waitress off.

"What is the *humph* for?" Lydia asked.

"So, you like him?"

"He's attractive."

A smile broke out across Mayor Mason's face. "So, you're attracted to him? Ethan Young?"

Lydia moaned. "I'm not saying that. I'm just saying what is obvious to anyone who looks at him."

The Mayor raised her eyebrow. "I have to tell you; I find it funny. You were looking for something different and left Sweet Blooms to find it, and the only guy that ever makes it back home so I can see them is someone who was born here?"

"I can see the irony of it all," Lydia groaned. "But let's keep this in mind. I'm just saying he's attractive. I haven't said I'm committing to him or that he's a potential husband. Let's not overemphasize what is just a commentary on the fact that he was born handsome."

"You two could be cute together."

"How can you make that jump? I just met him!"

The Mayor grinned. "You are so passionate. Hear me out. I may not do a lot of things well, and we don't have the best relationship, but I know you. If you've stayed in his presence this long, there's something there. If you would walk away from doing pro bono legal work and take a break with him, then yes, there is something there. I'm your mother. I know."

Lydia sat back and shook her head.

"Me and Ethan? One of us would kill the other one if we stayed in the room for too long. It doesn't even bear thinking what would happen if we tried to have a relationship."

"I was surprised you wanted to meet here," Ethan said as they walked into the community center.

"When you saw me yesterday, I was using two offices that would normally be rented out. The community center is where we hold classes for the community. We rent the bottom floors because they aren't in demand." Lydia said as she walked across the floor. "We've got a total of five rooms down here."

"I can see why it's not in demand. It's a bit dreary, don't you think?"

Lydia shrugged. "This is what we could afford. There's also not a huge selection when you tell people you're not sure how many people will show up or from where. Your in-town options go down because a lot of businesses serve as their business and their home."

"It's hard to educate if you don't have space," Ethan murmured.

"That is so true," Lydia said with a grin. "When we manage to convince people to come to Sweet Blooms, they need to be put up, and we need to make sure we have a good showing of people. We've invited people, and if enough people don't show up, then the teachers don't come back. We recently discovered there is a whole community of people who know how to do woodworking. Adam Cade brought them to our attention, but as you may know, a lot of them are on the outskirts. We're trying to inform them about their earning potential."

Ethan followed her as she walked into the first room. Ethan had wanted to see what the courthouse was doing to help the citizens of Sweet Blooms. He was convinced that it was going to be a short, uninformative visit. Ethan was wrong.

Lydia explained the various classes that were offered. She taught classes on personal finance, wills and small businesses. She also explained that it was a challenge to get the information out to everyone. Having the people in Sweet Blooms live so far apart made it harder to get information and help to everyone.

Ethan walked into the next room and saw the classroom setup. "And your attendance for your last classes, how did that go?"

Lydia shook her head. "I have to tell you; a lot of our classes are done one-on-one by going to people's homes. But we still pay to have this space at the community center."

Ethan looked around the main room and noticed there was a refrigerator. When he opened it, it was filled with plates of food. He looked over his shoulder at Lydia.

"What's this about?" he asked.

"There's a fee for all of our classes, but some people don't have the fee. They do have food, and that food is taken in trade for the services. I make sure it's distributed to the people who can't cook for themselves and for the staff who work late."

"How long has this program been set up?"

"I started it when I came home a couple of years ago."

Ethan followed her around as she explained what each room was for. He pictured her teaching the classes and recruiting for those classes, and he smiled. Ethan wasn't sure about the people in Sweet Blooms, but he was getting a very clear picture of the nature of Lydia.

"A lot of people start things, but it takes a different, more committed person to see it through," he said.

"If I had heard that last week, I would have thought you were making fun of me. Now, I'm starting to think there's more to you than I originally thought. So, I have to ask. Can you really just leave your home and come here to Sweet Blooms?"

Ethan smiled. "I don't really have a place that I go to. I own a lot of houses and what I do is rent them out. Sometimes I keep an attic or basement apartment that would be too much trouble to rent for myself. I use those for times when I'm coming through town. So, to answer your question, there is no home for me to go back to."

Ethan knew what she was asking. In an odd way, it was the question his father had asked him the day he walked away. Home was such a loaded word. For so long it was associated with his past and not a place at all. He was in his thirties, and he was willing to admit that the idea of putting down roots and creating a home had died for him the day his dad had closed the front door on him. There had been women who were convinced they could create a home with him, but it didn't last. They saw him as he was and never got to know the boy from the outskirts. He'd accomplished what he set out to do, but he couldn't find anyone to share it with.

"Well, I'll do my best to make sure you get to see what we really look like."

"In spite of how this may end, I want to say to you now, thank you."

"For?"

"For taking the time to see the man and not just the boy from the outskirts."

Ethan received a text from Lydia telling him her address. After going through the community center today, Lydia mentioned she had a client to meet. She wanted to introduce him around Sweet Blooms tomorrow. In preparation, she wanted to meet with him this evening. When Ethan arrived at the house, it wasn't what he was expecting at all.

The address led him to a winding driveway that was bordered on both sides with floral bushes that popped full of color. When his car arrived at the house, he immediately thought it looked like a life-size gingerbread house. He wanted to smile at how whimsical the house looked. The lawn was neatly cut and had small stone statues of fairies and gnomes in the garden. He looked up at the house itself, where fairies sat atop the gutters.

As he walked up the three steps, little lights went off. He wasn't sure what to expect when the door opened.

"I'm glad you made it. Come in."

Ethan braced himself for the interior. There wasn't a need. When he walked past her into the house, it looked like every other house—a dining room to the right, a living room with a television and mini bar in front of him, and to the left, he would guess the kitchen.

"Are you okay, Ethan?"

He looked over his shoulder and then turned to face her. She laughed.

"Ah, I understand. I keep forgetting you don't live in town and this probably started after you had left. Every year the nearby college does a theme contest to raise money. I am one of the three houses that gets a "makeover" by one of three students. As you can see, my student had fairy tales."

Ethan laughed. "Well then, yes, that makes it all clear now."

"Please take a seat."

Ethan took a seat in what his dad would have called the TV chair. It was large and comfy. It had a plaid pattern and, most important, on the armrest was a remote holder and in it was a romance book and a bag that said nails and things. Lydia sat across from him on the sofa and pulled her legs up, sitting Indian style.

When he saw her on the couch alone, he got ready to move, and she held out her hand to stop him.

"No, please stay where you are. I think this conversation is going to be awkward enough," she said.

Ethan could see her fidgeting in her seat, and it distressed him on a level he wasn't used to. Was she rethinking showing him around? "Did you have second thoughts?"

Lydia shook her head. "I have been thinking, and I think it's best if we continue the way we've started. I want to make sure you know why people may look at us oddly, and it has little to do with you."

When he had left her, she had still been in her work wear. Now she had on jeans and a tee shirt that said: Lawyers do it for justice. He was in a new position. He couldn't remember the last time he had wanted to comfort someone. He wasn't the touchy-feely type. Most situations Ethan thought could be fixed with money. This was definitely not one of those times, and it left him in a state that he was completely unfamiliar with—helpless.

"So, there's nothing traumatic I need to tell you. I've been in a relationship before, and I've been engaged as well. However, my last relationship was here in town, and it was a public affair. Since we will be posing as a couple, I thought it was only fair to let you know what had happened."

Ethan reached out. "You don't need to tell me a thing. This thing between us isn't real, and I've had my share of horror stories."

Lydia smiled. "Thanks, but I'd rather head off any gossip rather than you hear it from wherever."

"I don't know. If you feel you need to tell me this story, doesn't this go contrary to the whole *Sweet Blooms is a nice place that can take care of itself* thing?"

Lydia shook her head. "All towns need actors. A gossip or two does not destroy a town. Think of gossips like rotten food in compost. You may not like it when they arrive, but they can do some good in the end." She readjusted on her cushion of the couch. "So here goes," she said. Ethan could see she was looking right over his shoulder. "I met a man during my last year of law school. He was good looking and hadn't decided what he was going to specialize in. In fact, he presented himself in such a way that it appeared he would give up the city and move to Sweet Blooms with me to do work here."

"Not so bad."

Lydia swallowed and blinked hard a couple of times. "I didn't think so at the time either. He came to town and looked it over and thought it would be great for us to work together in town. He asked me to marry him. I accepted."

"You're doing fine."

Lydia nodded. "We got ready to open a business in town. He thought we should wait a year to marry. We could save up, and in the meantime, we could open a practice. It was all going okay until we took the business certificate to the courthouse and my mother refused to sign it."

Ethan was confused. "She refused to sign it because…?"

"It was her opinion that he wasn't with me for me. She offered to issue the license as long as it had my maiden name on it. He could wait a year if he wanted to and we could open it with both our names on it at that point."

Ethan knew what was coming, and he felt for the idealistic young woman who was still in school. "Let me guess, he was a gold digger. Looking to put his name on something so he could keep it or bargain with it," he said.

Lydia nodded. "Unfortunately, he hadn't done his research. He just got to the part where I was the Mayor's daughter. He also saw the part that said Sweet Blooms was worth a lot of money in land, but he didn't look at the books. I was naïve and impressionable at the time."

Ethan looked at Lydia sitting proudly on the couch, and for once he wanted to ask her what her ex's name was so he could give her the justice she deserved. She hadn't said anything bad about him. Even now, she owned this incident as if it were all her doing.

"There's no shame in trusting people who should love you."

Lydia stared at him in wonder. "You are definitely not what I was expecting, Ethan Young. I thank you for that."

He nodded. "So, I can guess, the way this story is going, that while you may have had high hopes, your mother was not moved."

Lydia nodded. "You would be right. However, he wouldn't go away after that. He thought to get the town's sympathy, and so what had been a personal affair became an exploration by the town to determine if a man would want to be with Mayor Mason's daughter, who happened to be impulsive and bull-headed."

Ethan thought about what she must have endured. He was born in the outskirts, and when he was ready, he left. Lydia wouldn't have had those same options. She had stayed in town after the gossip.

"Even after that, you see the good in Sweet Blooms?"

Lydia managed a smile. "Especially after that. I have to say that a small town has a way of helping you find what you're made of Ethan, small towns are like family. They help you to find yourself, and they show up when you need help."

"And they helped you?"

"When we first arrived, everyone welcomed him, but then when they all knew he was a gold digger, everyone banded together to get rid of him. The hotel was full, and he needed a reservation to eat anywhere, including the Banter House."

They both laughed at that. When the laughing subsided, Lydia pushed on.

"This is why us pretending to be together will fix several problems on both of our sides."

"What problems?"

"You can do the right thing and give the deeds back to the city instead of getting revenge on the whole city."

"I'm trying to save the city, yet it's considered revenge?"

"You're saving the city to lord it over them. To say a person from the outskirts saved them."

"Does it matter where I'm from?"

"Does it? If it doesn't, you could keep the ownership and put it in a trust or company name."

Ethan thought about it. "I already agreed that if you could show me this better, nicer Sweet Blooms, I'd meet you halfway."

Lydia smiled. "Lastly, there is a benefit for me."

Ethan frowned. "Besides being able to say you were the one who saved the town from the outskirter?"

"That was uncalled for."

Ethan sighed. "You're right. I guess I was testier than I thought."

"I won't be the pity case either."

"The pity case?"

"I will have recovered by bringing home a new man who isn't a gold digger."

Ethan laughed. "At this rate, you might be considered the gold digger."

Lydia paused. "How much money do you have?"

Ethan smiled. "A man never speaks of these things. I have enough."

"Well, be that as it may, this will be a win-win situation."

"All of this from being in a fake relationship with you, counselor?"

"Yeah, all that and a bag of chips."

Ethan nodded. He held out his hand "To us both being enlightened."

Lydia grabbed his hand. "To enlightenment."

They both stood up, and Ethan looked around. "Does this mean I get to spend the night?"

Lydia smiled and guided him to the front door. "It means you get to bring me breakfast in the morning. I like egg whites on a toasted roll, with bacon and orange juice with no pulp. I'll see you in the morning at eight."

Ethan stood outside looking at the closed door. He felt the excitement of a new adventure. He reveled in it. It wasn't until then that Ethan remembered. He hadn't felt anything close to excitement in a while, and no woman had piqued his interest like Lydia. He always went with his gut and right now his instincts were saying this could be fore than a ruse. It could be real.

Five

Ethan woke up to silence and thought he had been kidnapped. The city was always moving and waking up to darkness was a jolt. Two hours later, the birds began to sing. By five, he had already made six calls and had a conference call. Sweet Blooms didn't wake up until six, but deals were happening 24/7. After getting past the jolt of silence, he got up, ordered Lydia's breakfast, and made it to her house at eight on the dot.

When he arrived in his truck, she was already walking out the door. She got in on the passenger side and held out her hand for the roll.

"Good morning to you too. I didn't know I was the chauffeur for the day," he said with a grin.

Lydia opened the roll and took a bite. "Good morning," she said, covering her mouth with her hand. "I promise I'll be human once I get the first cup of coffee in me."

"Ahh, you're one of those."

Lydia glared at him over her roll. "I can't debate the benefits of coffee until I've had my cup."

Ethan laughed and drove to the courthouse.

When they arrived, he followed her to her office. As he was about to ask a question, she shook her head no.

"Give me five minutes," she said.

A few minutes later she came back into the room with a smile and a cup in her hand.

"Thank you. Now we can start."

Ethan couldn't help but laugh. "I can't even imagine what you would do in my world."

"You mean they work before coffee?" she said in exaggerated horror.

"I'm trying to find a time when they don't work. What's on today's agenda?"

"Well, I thought I'd introduce you to people who I know, and I'd show you the kinder part of Sweet Blooms. I realize you probably lived and went to school in the outskirts."

Ethan nodded. "When I went to school. There wasn't anyone to help us on the farm when we could farm. And no one came looking for an outskirt kid."

Lydia reached out and touched his arm. "We do things differently now. We may not be the most fiscally evolved group, but we are doing better with taking care of what we think is our greatest treasure."

Ethan looked at her skeptically. "That would be?"

"Our kids," Lydia said with a smile. "Let's go to the morning event."

Ethan followed Lydia out of the courthouse to a shop called Sweet Blooms. The smell of candy accosted him as he walked into the shop. Lydia must have been here before because she didn't even stop in the candy haven. Instead, she walked through another door that was held open by a man.

"Welcome to Sweet Blooms," he said.

Sweet Attractions

Lydia looked over her shoulder and beckoned Ethan. "Come on, we don't want to be late." Ethan didn't question her, he just followed. They walked through what looked like a 1950s ice cream parlor. The floor was covered in black and white squares. The tables were a combination of benches and booths, and at the counter, there were pumps dispensing soda and ice cream. He thought Lydia would stop here, but she went through a set of open doors at the end of the room.

The doors led to a paradise.

It was an attached garden, and all-around children ran and played. The adults were walking up and down aisles that had tables filled with sweets and tongs so people could select the tasty morsels into plastic bags to be weighed. on the side filling their bags with food.

Lydia turned towards him. "Welcome, Ethan. I know you think Sweet Blooms doesn't care, but one of the many things I noticed when I came home was there was a hunger problem in our town. The farmers had food most of the time, but there were seasons they just didn't make ends meet. Their children were suffering from it.

All of the businesses donate money or food to this event, and it's held every two weeks. The parents come and pick up food while the children get food to eat."

Ethan looked around and saw a couple or two from the outskirts. They stood right next to the other parents who were there. He thought about his childhood. There had been hard times, and when his dad heard that there was a family in need, everyone tried to help out as much as they could. He looked at Lydia standing next to him.

"So, who started this program?"

Lydia looked at him. "It was one of the new initiatives that was started in the last couple of years. We've been looking at the community to find out what is needed and how we can all work together."

Lydia left him and went to play with the kids. An older woman walked up beside him.

"You Barrick's boy?"

Ethan turned to look at an older woman who was looking up at him expectantly. He looked around to see if anyone else had heard before he answered.

"Yes."

"You got the look of him."

Ethan wasn't sure what the older woman wanted, but he had patience. She was also one of the first people to actually recognize him.

"I'm sorry. I don't know your name."

"My name is Rose. Its what people call me anyway. I see you here with Lydia."

Ethan smiled. Lydia was right; memories were long.

"Don't be putting me in the same boat as everyone else. I just want to make sure you're really here for Lydia, and you can appreciate her."

Ethan gave Rose a longer look. "I'm good to all women."

Rose tapped him on the head. "I'm not saying you have no breeding. I'm saying Lydia is special. I hope you can recognize how special she is."

Ethan nodded to the older woman. "I see it."

"Not so much, but you will." Rose turned from him, and Ethan called out.

"Excuse me, ma'am, if you don't mind me asking, how did you know I was Barrick's son? No one else seems to know."

Rose laughed. "Ethan, I see true. I see who you are, not who I need you to be. People look at you and see what they need, not who you are. You need to learn that; it'll help you to live a more peaceful life."

Lydia touched his shoulder and brought his focus back to her. "Ethan, are you okay?"

He looked at Lydia. Her hair was disheveled, and he could see there were some daisy petals in her hair. Her cheeks had a glow to them, and her smile called to him to play.

He took her hand. "I'm getting there. What else is going on?"

"The kids play for another hour or until their parents come back. Rose has opened up the maze. Let's go."

Lydia dragged him along, but he had to admit he would have followed her no matter what. Maybe he had judged Sweet Blooms and its residents too soon.

"Oh, this must be a big one," Yolanda said as Lydia closed the door to their shared office. She grinned, holding her box of Godiva chocolates in her hands. "I'm sitting here, and you come to deliver a golden box of happiness to me. What Latina could say no?"

Lydia had been friends with Yolanda for the last six years. She'd met her during a summer program before they both applied to law school. Lydia sat in front of the desk and tapped the golden box.

Yolanda opened the box and looked inside before she meticulously picked one and popped it into her mouth. "I'm not sure what this is for, but you've got it."

"I need your logic and clarity. This won't be a regular thing, so enjoy the box."

Yolanda continued to eat the chocolate and closed her eyes as she swallowed another one.

"Okay, I've been sufficiently paid. Although you must know that I would have given it to you for free."

"I know." Lydia looked at her friend. "It's not that I don't think you'd do it. I just want us to make sure we're on the same page of how serious I see this," she said, realizing that Yolanda could have taken the whole giving her a present to do this task wrong. Lydia reached out and put her hand over Yolanda's. "You know—"

Yolanda reached forward and stopped her from talking. "Stop. This is obviously something big. You've given a golden box, and I'll give you the full benefit of logical brain. Ask away and be done."

The time was here, and Lydia didn't feel ready to ask the questions she needed to. She was losing her perspective, and she needed someone in her corner. Yolanda had been a friend through it all. She had been around when she'd made the first mistake. She wanted someone who would have the history and not be biased against her.

"Well, here goes," Lydia said.

"Get to it. I'm already through half the box, and we're still playing footsy."

"Ethan Young."

"The hot guy who came in on the pro bono day?"

"Yes, well, I'm showing him the good in Sweet Blooms, so he'll want to give the deeds back to the town."

Yolanda leaned on the desk. "You sure you want to

ask me anything, because I can see some problems right now. Maybe the best person to ask these kinds of questions to is your mother?"

"That is the last resort," Lydia said. "My first thought was that I should ask you first in the hopes of getting a fair shake."

"Okay, go for it."

Lydia took a deep breath and blew it out, squared her shoulders, and sat back in the chair. "I decided to pretend to have a relationship with Ethan so I could show him the good in Sweet Blooms. Now he's turning into a nice guy. I'm thinking, should I ditch the plan or…?"

Yolanda popped the last candy in her mouth and licked all of her fingers. She was sure she had never seen Yolanda do anything like this in her life.

"Showing him the good in Sweet Blooms is one thing. But you volunteered to serve it up with a side of fake relationship?"

"Yes."

"Ethan Young, Mr. Hot and Single, with swag pouring off of him as he walks?"

Lydia nodded. "He was so determined to save the town and let everyone know it was an outskirter who did it. It would have been a slap in the face to the people who have a problem with them and discredited the people who never had an issue. It would tear the town apart."

"Not to mention it would be an issue for your mother." Yolanda cleared her throat and sat up a little taller. "Well, if you need to fake a relationship with someone, he's definitely on the top of the list."

"I didn't suggest it for that reason."

Yolanda held up her hands. "I get it. You were probably caught up in the moment and did what you thought would be the best thing for everyone."

Lydia sighed. "Really? For a moment you sounded like my mom. All the things I do seem to be based on a deeply passionate nature. The height of foolishness run amok."

"Listen, it's true you are usually the first one to take the hill, but you don't do it foolishly," Yolanda said. "I heard you say the word passionate several times, and you make it seem like it's a curse. You know that your passion is what others look for. Don't turn your back on what I think is a natural gift. Now, all that being said, we both know you aren't asking me about saving Sweet Blooms. You're asking me to sign off on a possible decision."

"I was a fool before. I was a fool in public. How can I be sure that I'm not heading down that road again?"

Yolanda smiled. "I can see you've been thinking on this issue. If you have, then you know that there are no guarantees when it comes to humans. But if it's any consolation, you've got a good eye looking at Ethan."

"You know it's not just his looks."

"Maybe not, but they sure don't hurt."

Lydia laughed. "I'm not expecting him to fall in love with me. I think I just want to choose a person who wants to be with me."

"I hear you," Yolanda said. "So, it seems like you have a handle on what you're doing and you know why you're doing it. What do you need from me?"

"I'm scared," Lydia confessed. "If I'm scared, isn't that a warning sign not to do it?"

Yolanda reached out and covered Lydia's hands. "Stop over thinking this. I don't know the future. No one knows the future. Life is meant to be lived. Don't doubt that you deserve to be living it too."

Lydia laughed. "That's why you're the best. I knew you'd help me see straight."

Yolanda laughed. "Trust yourself, Lydia. Your instincts are good."

"Really?"

Yolanda looked forlornly at the empty Godiva box. "Well, at the very least, you know how to go for the lookers."

Lydia thought making a decision to work with Ethan to save the town would put her mind at ease. She was wrong. She went to work after meeting with Yolanda and found she could barely function. She kept looking at the door waiting for Ethan to show up.

What was he doing anyway? Lydia knew she was impatient, but now that she had come to a decision, she wanted to share it and move on it. Needless to say, the day went by slowly and poorly because he didn't show up.

When the next morning came, of course, he showed up at her door looking refreshed. He was dressed in a blue cotton shirt and dark blue pants. He had on fingerless gloves as well. She didn't know why, but she was in no mood to ask questions either.

"It's my day off," Lydia grumbled. "I'm sorry. I should have told you that I alternate with Yolanda, and this week, Wednesday is my day off."

Ethan smiled. "I know. You know we really have to work on this whole you not being a morning person thing."

Lydia sighed. "There's nothing to work on. Bring a morning offering for happier service. I feel like this isn't an I was just in the neighborhood call."

"No, it's not."

Lydia shook her head. "Come on in." He walked into the house, and she pointed to the sofa. "Sit." She knew she sounded abrupt, but she just needed her coffee. That would make it better. If Ethan was going to be around her for any amount of time, he should be able to deal with this part of her personality.

She walked into her kitchen where directly on the left was a counter with her coffee pot on it. It had an automatic timer. She waited patiently, and then the telltale ding of the bell went off. A moment later the sweet symphony of coffee filling a cup could be heard. It was followed by the deep aroma of rich coffee. She didn't need sugar or cream. Lydia picked up the cup from the coffee machine and held the mug as if it held gold. After a few sips, she opened her eyes and walked back towards the living room.

She took a seat on the couch opposite Ethan and sighed. She was ready to deal with the world now.

"Good morning, Ethan."

He was looking at her with a raised eyebrow and an amused expression. "Can I speak to the real Lydia Mason now?"

She snuggled the cup closer to her chest. "I'm afraid this is her. You'll have to take it or leave it. I hope there was something very important for you to have come over this morning."

"You get a little snippy when you're caught unprepared."

"I'm not unprepared. You were unexpected."

He grinned. "I can see how you might make a distinction, although there is no difference."

"I'm not going to argue with you on why I'm right," she snapped.

Holding up his hands, he looked at her. "Okay, you're right. You're the lawyer. I'm not here to fight."

"Why are you here?"

"I'm here to do my part in our relationship."

"Excuse me?" Lydia said incredulously. Certainly, she had heard him wrong. "What exactly would you need to do?"

"Come out with me for a bit. I'll bring you back," he said.

Lydia was curious and cautious at the same time. "Where are we going?"

"I'm taking my girl out, outskirt style."

Lydia looked at him and curiosity had her going to put on blue jeans and a tee shirt. She felt a little underdressed around him, but when she came out, he didn't mention if he thought she was underdressed.

They got into his truck, and he drove for about thirty minutes in silence. Finally, he pulled onto a side road.

"I want you to know I'm not into exploring a kissing site," Lydia said.

Ethan smirked. "I don't know, Lydia; every day it seems like your opinion of me is slipping."

"I'm just saying." Lydia ignored the chuckles she heard and got out of the truck. She walked to the front of the truck, and Ethan held out his hand.

"Come on, city girl. I want to share a moment with you." She placed her hand in his and went with him. As they walked down the dirt path, Lydia saw it open up into a clearing with a large pond. She gasped.

"I didn't know this was here," she said, looking at Ethan.

Ethan smiled. "Every person in the outskirts knows this pond is here. It's a popular date spot."

Lydia looked around the lush area and then turned back to Ethan.

"It's pretty, and the area is quiet, but a date spot? I'm not seeing it."

Ethan walked her to the side of the pond where there was a blanket and a tackle box.

"You need to see with outskirter eyes," he teased.

He picked up the box and walked them over to two boulders where there were two fishing poles.

"We bring our dates here to fish. The way it goes is, we see what she can do, and then we get an idea of what kind of girlfriend and potential wife she'd make."

Lydia picked up the fishing rod and then found the hook. "I've fished before, but I don't like baiting the hook. I don't like killing stuff."

Ethan opened the box and gave her some moldy bread. "We don't use live bait. We use bread."

Lydia smiled at Ethan. "That is so considerate of you."

Ethan laughed. "It's not considerate. Worms are too valuable. We need them in the earth to work the soil. So, we don't use worms for fishing. In fact, some of the girls who want to really impress a guy wouldn't even bother to use the rod. They'd go out there and grab them with a net. That's how you can tell you've got yourself a keeper."

Lydia looked at him and laughed. "Well, if that is the baseline, you're going to have to look somewhere else. I've never fished unless it was in a market, and as pretty as the pond is, I don't think I'll be putting my feet in that water."

He reached over and took the rod from her hand and helped her down the boulders. "Let's talk."

"Is that code for I failed?"

His tone was calm, and he guided her back to the blanket, all the while telling her things about the trees and the birds they saw. She let the sound of his voice seep into her. He was so easy to talk to that this had to be right.

"You worry a lot about failing or not living up to some standard."

"Yes," she replied sadly. "It's part of being the mayor's daughter."

"There had to be a time when she wasn't the mayor."

Lydia smiled. "There was. There was also a time when she was a housewife, if you could believe it."

They both sat down, and he pulled out a bag of chips. When she saw the chips, she had to hold in a laugh.

Ethan saw her and laughed first. "Go ahead and laugh. I told you this was an outskirters date. That means it's got to be practical and inexpensive. If I bought a whole lot of food, you might think I was going to do that all of the time. I don't want to give the wrong impression."

Lydia shook her head. "Dating outskirter style doesn't seem as fun as I thought it would be."

Ethan raised an eyebrow. "You thought about dating an outskirter?"

"Let's say it was one of those things we put on the list of what the brave and cool girls would do."

"Ah, so you all were admiring from afar."

She blinked. "Don't let it go to your head. We were young, and I guarantee you none of us thought we'd have to do any fishing."

"Outskirters are an honest lot," he said.

Lydia shook her head. "No, people are an honest lot, Ethan, even the people from Sweet Blooms."

He didn't naysay her he just looked at her. After a few moments under that dark, seeking gaze, Lydia turned away.

"I think you're honest, Lydia Mason," he said. "In fact, I think you are one of the realest people I've met in a while."

She was uncomfortable being in the spotlight, and his comments didn't make it any easier. "Stick with me, Ethan, and I'll show you a whole town of real people."

He reached out and tilted her chin towards him. "I'm honest too. I'm honest enough to say I like you, Lydia Mason. I don't know if I'll buy into the town thing, but you are definitely a surprise, and not much surprises me anymore."

Before she could come up with a response, he leaned in and kissed her. Could it be the mayor's daughter was sitting on a blanket being kissed by Ethan Young? Yes.

She thought he was going to be quick and hasty storm the castle, but it turned out his mouth lightly touched hers. He brushed by her lips and pulled back so their eyes could meet. She licked her lips, and his eyes followed the movement.

She could feel her heart racing in her chest. There was an excitement that lingered between them that was palatable in the air. Had he been thinking about kissing her as much as she had him. If this was what anticipation did, she was all for it. When his head came down, she expected another kiss. Instead, he just laid his forehead against hers.

"I think this date is over," he murmured.

"Really?" Her voice came unsteadily.

"Don't sound like that."

"Like what?"

"Like you wouldn't mind it if I kissed you again."

She lifted her eyes up to his, and before either one of them could speak, they both heard the deep barreled voice of Barrick Young.

"This must be what they call slumming now."

Six

Ethan groaned aloud at the sound of his father's voice. He looked at the wide-eyed Lydia and then dug into his pocket.

"Lydia, this is going to be unpleasant I'm sure, take my truck. Stay on the main path; it will take you to the Cade's place. Do you know where that is?"

She nodded, but it was as if in slow motion. Then she spoke. "You want me to leave you?"

"Yes, my dad just comes here to think but I don't want you to be here just in case me and him have to walk down memory lane. When we go down memory lane it feels more like memory alley. I'll be fine."

She looked around. "Do you want—"

He placed his hand on hers and smiled. "No, I've got it. I'll see you later."

She nodded and walked out of the clearing and right past his father. She nodded as she passed, and his father grunted. When she was out of the clearing, Ethan spoke.

"Dad."

Barrick walked towards him, he looked at the blanket and then circled to the boulders. Ethan looked at his dad and thought, if this is what I'll look like later,

I'll take it. His father had aged, but he was still a powerful man.

As his father came back towards him, Ethan could still feel that sense of pride and respect he had for his dad. To him, his dad was still the one who was able to make magic happen. He might have gone to school to learn things, but Ethan was sure there were things his dad knew that no school knew.

Barrick stood in front of him, legs hip-width apart, with his arms crossed over his chest. "Don't you think you're a little old to be bringing dates here?"

Ethan was confused by the question because he was so wrapped up in seeing his father. A moment later, he realized what his dad was talking about.

"I have an arrangement with Lydia—"

His dad held up both hands. "I don't need to know what you all call it today. I'm just saying I think you make enough to be able to take a woman somewhere."

Ethan looked at the situation and decided it would be futile to explain. He couldn't defend what was going on, so he went on the attack.

"Maybe I should be asking you why you're out here," Ethan muttered. Then he looked around as if he were really searching. "Maybe you're trying to throw me off the real goal. Could it be you have a female friend you're bringing to the pond?"

"I'm here to think. I've got no time for women folk. I have to work on me."

Ethan stopped and heard what his father was saying, and for once he started to really see his dad. There was grey around his temple, and there were more worry lines than laugh lines on his face.

"What's wrong, dad?"

Barrick stood as tall as he could and looked Ethan in the face. "I'm not asking for any money."

"I know that. I'm just asking if there's a problem," Ethan replied. "Look, I'm not saying it's something you can't handle. What I'm saying is, if I can do something and you'd let me, I'd like to help."

Barrick waved him away and turned. "Things are changing. The land is getting smaller each year. The glade is eating it up. Eventually, there won't be much of anything left."

"We're a family, dad. You know you can depend on me."

Barrick sighed. "Family? You haven't been home in years."

"It doesn't matter. We're still family."

Barrick's chin lifted. "You depended on me all your life."

"And you never disappointed. I'm just saying I'm here."

Barrick nodded and then turned to leave.

"Dad, you're not staying?"

Barrick shook his head. "No, if I don't walk into the peace, I won't find any." Barrick turned to go, and Ethan ran after him.

"I need a ride."

Barrick looked him over and kept walking. "I'll take you back, but I should leave you here. I mean, who gives a woman the keys to his truck? She's probably left it at the mechanic, and they're figuring out how much it's worth."

Ethan laughed. "I'm sure the truck will be fine."

Barrick shook his head. "That's what they all say until they have no truck."

Sweet Attractions

"We were delighted to see you at our event to—" said the answering machine. Mayor Mara Mason turned it off before the message could finish. She didn't need to hear the rest of it. Of course, they were happy to see her. She had a donation check with their name on it.

She sat down on her couch with a weary sigh. She glanced across the living room to her friend Charles as he brought the tray in for them to have coffee.

"Your patience is thin today, Mara," Charles Lyndham said. He lived in the apartment above the mayor and years ago they had settled into a routine that consisted of him driving her home every day. While the town thought he did it for security, both of them had started it as a matter of convenience. Over the years they had become good friends.

Mara looked at Charles and contemplated his words. She was a middle-aged woman who held the title of mayor in a small town that was being dragged, kicking and screaming, into the future. Most of all, she was the mother of a beautiful woman who, for all accounts, couldn't stand her.

Mara sat across from Charles in her eat-in kitchen. She had a small table and two chairs. The tray took up almost all of the surface area of the wooden tripod table. Like so many other parents, she couldn't recall exactly when things had changed. One day Lydia thought she was beauty incarnate, and the next she had become the enemy.

She glanced at Charles across her teacup. He was a lot like her, settled into her situation. Mara knew he had a son, but he never talked about him.

"What chance do you think I have of getting my daughter back?"

Charles waited, and for a moment Mara thought he wouldn't answer. "Opportunity is something we make, not something we wait to be delivered to us."

"What kind of cryptic answer is that?"

Charles continued to fix his coffee. After he had finished putting in his sugars and cream, he stirred and air toasted Mara. "I thought those were the safest words I could give you."

"You're not on duty. I'm not your boss, and I'd like my friend to answer."

"You already know the answer, Mara, and you don't like it."

She placed five cubes of sugar in her tea.

"Had I known you wanted sugar with a bit of tea, I would have gotten you a larger cup," Charles commented.

"Why do you think I hired you at the courthouse?"

Charles didn't answer; instead, he just looked at her as he sipped.

"It's not because there's anything of value in there, really. I have my office in there, and all of the other mayors had security at their courthouses and offices. I didn't want to look less."

"Lydia has never seen you as less."

"She doesn't want me," Mara said and then took a gulp of her tea. If Mara was honest, she would say that her biggest fear was that she wasn't sure Lydia still loved her.

"What do you say to her, Mara?"

Mara was confused by the question. "What do I say to her? What kind of question—is it another one of those questions that make no sense to anyone but you?"

"You said you went out to an early lunch."

"Yes, we went to a place I could do without."

"I hope you didn't tell her that," Charles said.

Mara put her cup down and looked at Charles. "I didn't tell her that I didn't like the restaurant, but I'm sure she knew. I think she picked it because she knew I wouldn't like it."

"And maybe that is the problem when the two of you meet. You never have anything nice to say to her. If you are always correcting and criticizing, why would you think she wants to be around you?"

"I want what's best for her."

Charles stood up and pushed his chair back in. "Listen, as a parent who has lost a child because I pushed him away, I know some things. When you speak, don't focus so much on trying to help them as much as you should just try and accept them."

Charles left her in her apartment. She sat at the table thinking about what Charles had said for almost an hour. She went into her living room and laid down on her couch. It was a habit she did as the days went on. She looked across to the wall where there was a picture of her smiling while standing next to a man. Once, she had been young and passionate like Lydia.

She'd known a man who'd swept her off her feet. He'd promised her the moon she had believed him. They'd run away together and married in Vegas. It was thrilling, and he was larger than life. Then she'd gotten pregnant and the passion faded away.

She never wanted Lydia to know the pain of someone suddenly not loving you one day. Mara wanted her daughter to be strong, secure, and independent. She never wanted her to know how love could break you when it wasn't returned.

Mara shifted her gaze to the picture of Lydia graduating law school. Lydia was next to her best friend Yolanda, and both of them had their hands raised in triumph. That's how she wanted Lydia to live—happy, strong, and triumphant.

The picture right beneath that one was in a heart-shaped picture frame. It was Lydia at three with her hair in two blonde pigtails. She was about to blow a kiss at Mara who had taken the picture.

Tears blurred her vision. There was no one to be strong for. She let the tears fall and roll down her cheek onto the couch.

She cleared her throat and wiped away the tears. She had indulged in a passionate, reckless love and received a gift beyond compare Lydia. Now she had no love, she had no daughter, and she was alone. She could reflect back on the past and see she had played a part in pushing Lydia away. She'd done it to help make her stronger, but she'd done it, nonetheless. Now she was the mayor of Sweet Blooms to some; she was a woman to have as a connection, but she'd give it all up to hear the three-year-old in that picture throw her a kiss and say, "I love you, mommy."

Seven

"Listen up, people," Lydia announced to the room full of volunteers. "You'll go to the back of the room and get an envelope. Inside the envelope, it will tell you where you will be working and what you will be doing. If you have any physical restrictions, let the ladies at the back table know and they will reassign you."

Lydia watched the volunteers anxiously go to the tables. There was a special sort of excitement and dread as they went to find their names. Today they'd all met at the Lansing farm.

Her thoughts were interrupted by Ethan clearing his throat. She turned to look at him and tried not to stare at just how good he looked in his jeans and tee shirt.

"Yes?" she said with a drawn-out expression.

"You asked me to come to his farm, but what is the end goal of all this?"

"Twice a year, we offer our services on smaller farms that have women who have no one to help them, or a downed family member, and they can't get their farm work done. Or we offer to those who may have land but for one reason or another couldn't buy any seed to put on the land."

"You do this for every farm?" he asked.

"Don't take that tone with me, Ethan. I know what you're asking, and yes, we go to outskirt farms too, if they will let us, but it's usually harder to get them to participate."

Lydia waited until it seemed like everyone had their assignments. She called out numbers and told them where to get into waiting vans and trucks. Everyone else was staying with her on the Lansing farm to do half an acre.

She'd already separated the equipment by the task. She could see people dragging themselves to pick up shovels and rakes. Then she noticed that as some of the women picked up their equipment, they smiled at Ethan. One of them made a show of bending over to tighten her shoes, all the while keeping eye contact with Ethan. Lydia sucked her teeth and shook her head. It was true—Ethan was a distraction in a suit or in jeans.

When one of the women called out to Ethan, asking if he needed help with any of the work today, Lydia replied, "Ethan will be with me all day. If he needs anything, I'll make sure to give it to him." Her mind was so wrapped up in these women who had joined just to get Ethan's attention that she was taken off guard by Ethan's words.

"I suppose you'll supply me anything but fresh-caught fish," he murmured in her ear as he went by to help the men create rows to plant on the acre. Her stomach fluttered inexplicably at his nearness and her skin buzzed from the touch of his breath on her neck. He turned then and winked at her.

She would have had to cover her mouth to contain the laugh that wanted to escape and his comment, but she was suddenly quite distracted by the way her body reacted to his actions. As Ethan worked, she saw the two women looking after him. When they noticed Lydia was looking at them, they turned to their bucket of dirt.

Lydia went to their side. "Ladies, do you need help?"

The woman who had bent over to give Ethan a better view of her assets said, "It doesn't make a lot of sense for us to put these worms in the dirt. I mean, worms find their way into dirt all the time, right?"

During every volunteer session, it was always something. She had attributed it to Ethan being in this event, but to be fair, there was always someone who wanted to volunteer but didn't want to get dirty. Then she gave the woman the smile she gave to the opposition, just before she made them an offer they couldn't really refuse, but didn't want to take.

"The Lansings normally run this farm with no help from anyone. The only reason we're here is that Mrs. Lansing just had a baby and her mother broke her hip. So, while she's helping her mother around with the broken hip, she mentioned she needed time to plant her half acre."

The women looked stunned and then nodded.

"So, you were asking about the worms. The issue is, you ladies would be right that worms will find their way back into the soil. So, the red worms are special because they irrigate the soil. We ordered these worms, and after the group creates the holes, you two will drop a scoop of worm-rich dirt into the hole and then we'll have the last group of people plant their saplings right on top of them."

She looked at the women and saw them looking over her shoulder. She knew Ethan was there, and she was even more annoyed that these women weren't here to help the cause but to help themselves if they could.

"You need to decide if you want to help or if you want to look good. You can decide to stay here and do the task at hand, or you can go back to the table and get a reassignment in town. But whatever you are going to do, you need to decide quickly so we don't waste time that we could be using to help others."

When Lydia finished, the women had wrapped their arms around themselves and had an air of shame about them. They couldn't even look up at Lydia.

The woman who had spoken before cleared her throat.

"We didn't know, okay?" said one woman. The other one who was with her didn't even respond to Lydia. She just turned around and then went back to the table.

Lydia shook her head. "No, it's not okay, but if you're willing to work, I'm willing to overlook this."

The remaining woman looked at her companion, leaving her, and then she looked at Lydia.

"I'm here to work. I'll get this done, no problem."

As Lydia walked away, Ethan fell in step beside her.

"Is that common?"

"It's something every year." She didn't say that having him on the team this year had spread like wildfire. That she understood how Ethan had inspired them to join the event. His muscled arms, broad shoulders, and long legs often crossed her mind as well.

"It was tactful without being mean."

Lydia looked at him. "Did you expect me to be mean?"

"I have been around a lot of people, and they all have their own way of managing people. Some people try to keep people in line with fear, and others try to create a team atmosphere. I was prepared for either one."

Lydia gave him a long look. "So, do you know either one of those women?"

"I've seen them in town before."

"I didn't know," she muttered. Lydia paused, trying to get past the gut punch from his statement. "Look, I didn't know you were already with someone when I proposed—"

He reached out and tucked her hair behind her ear. The simple gesture was enough to interrupt her thoughts. She wanted to lean into his hand and feel the warmth on her skin, but she waited. She waited to see what would come of it all after that last statement.

"I'm not dating, seeing, or even interested in anyone but you," he said with a grin. "Maybe I should be asking you what kind of person you think I am."

Lydia was stopped in her tracks and didn't know what to say. She could litigate in any courtroom, but when she was facing him, all of that know-how went out the window. He reminded her that she was a woman and suddenly she was hyper aware of how much taller he was than her. That only added to the effect.

She cleared her throat. "I'm sure you're a fine person, and this was just to clear the air."

His gaze settled on her and his grin got a little wider. "Since you covered that so nicely, I'll show you how to do this little field here."

"You'll show me," she mocked. "I can see you have a gym body, but I don't know that it can handle real work."

Ethan laughed. "Are you suggesting I've forgotten my roots?"

"Of course not, I'm suggesting you've gone soft under those gym curves."

Ethan grinned. "Oh, I know a dare when I hear one. Let's go, counsel. Let me show you how it's done."

Hours later, after the sun had gone down and everyone was tired, Ethan drove Lydia home in his truck. When the truck hit a bump, Lydia groaned.

"You alright over there, counsel?"

"Don't tease me. I don't have enough energy to fight back."

"If it makes you feel any better, I'm hurting too."

"No, it doesn't," she chuckled. "It hurts to laugh."

"Why didn't you stop earlier if you were in pain?"

Lydia scoffed. "I wasn't in pain as long as I was looking at you. It was when the acre was done that it all hit me. You could have done the gentlemanly thing and stopped."

"Then how would I be able to look you in the face then?"

Finally, they made it to her place, and she stood at the door. The walkway was lit up with fairies.

"By the way, I think you'd always be able to look me in the face. You're a big boy. I think you can handle most things."

She wanted to pull back the words as soon as she said them. She was trying to show him the better part of Sweet Blooms, and fighting the reaction she had to him at the same time. Ethan Young was a temptation she hadn't expected so she did the only thing she knew how to do—she opened her front door to escape.

"Lydia?"

She turned around and found Ethan right next to her. "Ethan?"

"You're right. I can handle most things. You, on the other hand, are an unexpected surprise."

She opened her mouth to respond, and then he leaned in. He moved slowly to give her time to pull away, and a moment before their lips touched, he hesitated and looked her in the eye. Then his lips met hers, and lingered for a moment, brushing ever so slightly over them. He straightened up, and Lydia kept her lips pursed as if waiting.

"Good night, Lydia. I spoke the truth when I said I've never met a woman like you."

Lydia watched him get into his truck and drive away. When the truck was out of sight, she touched her mouth as if it had been her first kiss. The night air blew over her, and she looked at the empty street. How long had she been lost in the moment? She went inside, and before she fell asleep, she touched her lips again in wonder.

Ethan Young, you were not what I was expecting, was the last thought to cross her mind before she went to sleep that night.

Eight

It wasn't often that Mayor Mason visited the counsel area. Mara thought on what Charlie had said the other night and knew Lydia probably wouldn't be eager to see her either. She had been second guessing if she should have called or made an appointment. When she mentioned it to Charlie, he couldn't believe she had suggested making an appointment to see her daughter. So here she was about to open the door to her daughter's office, and once again, she wasn't sure what she was going to get. With her hand raised to knock on the door, it opened.

"Lydia?" Mara asked, looking at Lydia dressed in her suit with her suitcase in hand.

"Oh!" Lydia replied as she stepped out of the office and closed the door behind her. Mara backed up and gave her some room. She followed Lydia as she talked over her shoulder.

"I'm sorry I don't have time right now. I have an appointment. If you want, I can call you when I get back?"

"I thought we could—"

"And we can, just not right now." Mara followed her to the side exit of the building. When she got to the door, Lydia turned to her. "When I get back, I'll let you know." With those words, she got into her car and drove off.

Mara was jolted by the voice she heard next.

"So, it seems you are having trouble talking to your kid too. I guess being hard-headed isn't limited to certain people."

Mara turned to see Barrick. She could have walked away, but in the end, he was a part of the problem.

"Maybe it was a sign that it was time I went to the source," Mara said.

Barrick shrugged. "I'd be more open to talking if I had coffee."

"Really?"

"I wouldn't have asked if I didn't mean it."

Mara wanted to tell him too bad, but she thought about the news that had come to her regarding the farming and thought she could endure Barrick for Lydia's sake.

"Fortunately, for you, I'm in the mood for coffee as well."

They walked two blocks in silence. She found the little coffee shop and took a seat outside the store.

Barrick started the conversation. "I'm surprised. I was sure you wanted to hide me inside."

"There's no need to hide, and I don't think this will be a very long conversation. Why mess up a table?"

Mara watched Barrick pull the chair out and then lean his elbows on the table.

"What is it, Mayor?" Barrick asked snidely.

Mara raised her hand and signaled two coffees to the waitress.

"You didn't even ask what I wanted in mine."

"I didn't have to, Mr. Young. Contrary to what should be happening here, I'm paying for it. That means this whole event is free to you."

Barrick leaned back and looked at the Mayor. "I suppose you have the right of it. I'm listening."

"Are you aware that your son has bought a majority of the land in Sweet Blooms?"

Barrick laughed. "Ethan's a bit old to be telling me what he does with his money. If you say he's done it, I would believe it."

The waitress came and gave them their coffee. Mara nodded the woman off when it looked as though she was going to offer some pastries.

"Yes, well, I think it's a good idea for him to help, but it would be better for the town if he would give those deeds back to the town."

Barrick raised an eyebrow. "The boy knows how to handle his money. You want him to give you something he paid for?"

"In an ideal world, yes, but I know we don't live in one of those. I can give him a good price. We have been raising money for this, so no, he won't have a loss."

Barrick took a sip and looked around the street.

"I don't know, Mayor. Is it really bothering you that Ethan owns Sweet Blooms, or is it that an outskirter does?" he said.

Mara tilted her head to the side and then looked at Barrick.

"My concern is for the town. If any one person owns it, then the town will never be safe. It should be in a trust that no one can sell, to preserve the way it is. That being said, I will tell you that I think there is too much bad blood we haven't worked through for an outskirter to own Sweet Blooms."

Barrick stopped drinking his coffee and gave Mara another look.

"I didn't think you'd even admit to the problem."

Mara nodded to him. "I grew up here just like you did, Barrick. There has always been a separation between the two. I've also seen the plans that your son has brought. I think he has a plan that will bridge that section."

Barrick sat up in his chair and smiled.

"My boy is smart."

"He is. I think after seeing some of the projects that he has proposed come to light, there might be a day when we won't have people from Sweet Blooms and the outskirts. One day we might all be Sweet Bloomers."

Barrick shook his head. "I was with you until that last one. Me being a Bloomer? Not happening. Well, then I guess we're good."

"Not quite."

Barrick looked again at Mara.

Mara took a deep breath. She remembered what Charlie said, and she thought about how grown Lydia was and all that she had missed.

"I wanted to talk about your son and my daughter. It seems as though they have become an item lately."

Barrick sat back in his chair.

"Are you about to say something about how my boy may not be good enough for your daughter, Mayor?"

Mara heard the warning in his voice and held her ground.

"No, I'm not. I'm saying that Ethan isn't the type of man she normally dates. While I am the mayor of Sweet Blooms, I am also a mother."

Barrick didn't say anything; he just looked into his cup and then he finally broke his silence.

"You saying you think my boy may be good enough for your little girl?"

Mara tried to think about how she had even gotten to this table. No matter what Lydia thought, Mara knew she loved her beyond reason.

"I think that both of them are adults and we should be supportive and cautious when it comes to their feelings."

Barrick picked up his cup and chugged the rest of his coffee down. He wiped his mouth with the back of his hand and then leaned forward.

"I have to tell you that Ethan is a grown man. I don't get to tell him one way or another who he can and can't see. I lost that ability with him when he was twelve. That's assuming I ever really had that ability in the first place. What I can tell you is this—while you may have resolved that it's okay for them to be together, I'm not so sure."

Mara was taken aback by the words.

"You're not sure about what?"

"I'm not sure that your girl is the type of woman he needs."

There was no way to express the outrage and disbelief Mara was feeling.

"Really?"

Barrick sat back and held up his hands in front of him.

"Now hold on before you get all flustered. Ethan grew up with people who worked around him all the time.

I think your girl is smart, and she's pretty, but is she rugged enough to handle Ethan's ambition? You see, he owns parts of Sweet Blooms, and your daughter is working for you."

"She's a lawyer!"

Barrick shrugged. "She's a lawyer working for her mother. I know. I know she's your kid and she does no wrong. But I have to tell you this, Ms. Mayor, I won't interfere with Ethan's life. I'll even put in a good word because I think you're right that the town should own the land. Having things doesn't do anything but corrupt good people, and my son is a good man. But when it comes to long-term relationships, I don't know if your little girl has got what it takes to keep an outskirter man."

With those final words, he stood up and tipped his head before saying, "Hope you have a good day, and thanks for the coffee."

Lydia looked up at the door when she heard the knock. Yolanda poked her head in the room. Yolanda had that mischievous smile on her face. If Lydia was honest, she'd say that she'd been a little hesitant since she left her mother this morning. She had a will and last testament to go to, and one of the people in the will was not doing well. She had felt bad leaving her mother this morning, but at the same time, she was ashamed to admit she was relieved. Lydia knew she had only put off the meeting, but still, she was happy for any reprieve. Now it seemed like that reprieve might be over.

Yolanda's smile brightened when she spoke.

"There's someone here to see you."

Lydia sighed in defeat. "The Mayor, or my mother?" Yolanda was well aware of the relationship between her and her mother.

"Definitely not," Yolanda said as she walked in, and Ethan walked behind her.

Lydia saw Ethan smile and take a seat.

If she could package his smile alone, all of her negotiations would go smoothly. Watching Ethan was like watching a lion move. You couldn't say which part was the graceful part or the deadly part, but altogether it made an impressive picture. When she tried to focus just on his face, it didn't alleviate his power of enthrallment.

When did glasses become sexy? His face was well kept. He had the perfect beard, and she wasn't even a fan of the hair on the face trend. Then, in a last-ditch attempt to save herself and try to focus on whatever would come out of his mouth, her eyes fell to his lips. The last time he kissed her came back like a rolling wave, and the only thing that was on her mind was when he was going to do it again.

"How are you?" he asked as he took a seat. "I heard you were out earlier, so I thought I'd give it a try now."

"The day has been a busy one. I had to do a will, and the people aren't sure how long the loved one has."

"I'm sorry."

Lydia sighed. "You know what makes it sad is that it's a husband and wife. They've been together for fifty-eight years."

Ethan smiled. "That's a good run, they're really fortunate."

Lydia nodded. "The both of them are having health issues. It was so odd. I've visited both of them separately with their family members, and when they are apart, they are frail and sickly. Today they were brought together for the signing, and the both of them just perked up more than I've ever seen."

Ethan grinned. "They love each other. Love can hold a lot of things at bay or make your situation not so bleak."

"You sound like you speak from experience," Lydia said.

"No, not me, but I've seen it once or twice. Enough times for me to know that it's real, and I don't take it for granted. Love is a gift."

"You don't hear too many people saying that, and you definitely don't hear a lot of men saying that today."

Ethan shrugged. "I'm not the average bear."

"No, you're not."

"That's why I'm here, actually."

Lydia's body went from relaxed to tense. "Because?"

"I thought I'd come by your place tonight."

"Did you meet my mother on the way here? Is it going to be just you?"

Ethan laughed. "No, I didn't see your mother, it will just be me."

If he came by tonight, what would she cook? She tried to think about what the house looked like. Thank goodness the cleaning girl had come by. She didn't have to worry about that at least, and she supposed if she left the job about thirty minutes early, she could get…

"You've got to stop thinking that hard," Ethan said as he put his hand on his chest as if it were hurting him. "I can feel the thought waves assaulting me over here."

"Really? You just said—"

"I just asked if I could come over. I didn't ask you to cook. In fact, the whole point of tonight is for me to cook for you."

"What?"

He leaned on the desk and then laid his hand palm up in front of her. "Tonight, I'll be taking care of you," he said slowly. "Will you take a chance on me?"

Lydia looked at his opened palm, and she threw all of her doubts to the side and then placed her hand in his.

"So, what did you want me to provide for you? You know, for dinner?"

He grinned. "I'll bring everything, Lydia. The point is for you to relax, not to create more work for you. I'll assume you have nothing, so I'll be ready to come to your place say about seven?"

"So, you'll stop by around—"

"Come on, how about we say I'll be by at seven to cook for our date."

"Date?"

Ethan closed his hand over hers, and she could feel him stroking the top of her hand. It sent shivers across her skin.

"Yeah you know that thing that happens between two people who say they like each other," he said slowly.

The words made her breath hitch, and she licked her bottom lip in anticipation.

"I can see you have a way with words, Ethan."

"Don't worry, Lydia, I'm a man of my word. I'll deliver." With that, he stood up and brought her hand to his lips. "Until tonight."

He smiled and walked away. She had to hold her breath to make sure he was gone, and then she got up and closed the door. Leaning her forehead against the door, it came to her then. She and Ethan were dating, like a normal man and woman kind of dating.

The excuses were out of the way. This wasn't about saving Sweet Blooms. She knew Ethan was a good guy. She was sure he would do the right thing in the end. She was dating Ethan Young under false pretenses. She would tell him tonight that the charade was over. He wouldn't have to pretend he was in a relationship with the mayor's daughter.

Ethan was waiting for her at the house. As the sun began to set, he could see the magical little fairy lamps come on in her front yard. He had gone by the supermarket, so he had all the ingredients he needed to make dinner, and he'd brought a pot or two just in case. He wanted to make sure this was a night she wouldn't forget.

He had also bought some Nutella and a box of chocolates. He had seen the discarded Godiva boxes in Lydia's office. He was hoping if all went south, he would have at least those two items to redeem himself.

He'd received a call from the mayor saying she wanted to meet, but he wasn't going to bring that up tonight. Tonight, was about them.

Just when he thought she had been caught up at the office, she came around in her car. When she stepped out of it, she looked worn and tired. He hoped everything had gone okay with the older couple. Ethan knew that case really affected her. She had put her hair up in a ponytail, and she still had her suit on, but she had flip flops on her feet. He wouldn't have noticed, but her toes were painted Barbie pink. Ethan smiled. It seemed like there was so much more girly parts to Lydia that he couldn't wait to discover.

He got out of his car and pulled out the two bags. He looked over at her, and she stopped and gave a wan smile.

"I thought I would be able to beat you here," she said. He put down the bags and pulled out one of the three boxes.

"I bring gifts." Ethan held out the gold box. "And back-up Nutella if need be."

Lydia gave him a smile. "I can see you really do your research. I mean, how can I deny a man with these kinds of offerings?"

"I'm hoping you can't."

"Your foresight will profit you today, but I have to give you a disclaimer first, and then after that, we can see how you feel."

Ethan waited. He could see whatever she wanted to say was making her uncomfortable. She hadn't even invited him in yet.

"Tell me, although I should warn you not much can be said to dissuade me from tonight's date."

"Yeah, that's what I want to talk to you about, this date situation."

He watched her take a breath and then cross her arms over her chest.

"I don't think we should date," she said.

"Because?"

"Because it's not fair and I'm forcing myself on you."

Ethan smiled and then leaned against his truck. "You can't imagine how curious your words have made me. Tell me, Lydia, how are you forcing me?"

She looked so sincere and troubled.

"This whole thing about staying with me while we figure out the deeds."

"The deeds don't matter. I'm not one to let my feelings rule my decisions. My decisions about the deeds will be based on business, not feelings."

She looked taken aback.

"Well, the whole thing about you not telling anyone who you are and being my boyfriend. It's not right that you should be hiding yourself."

"I couldn't care less about the town. If they like me or if they don't, it doesn't really matter to me."

She put her hands on her hips.

"Well, maybe I want a guy that finds me, and we start dating because of what he thinks about me!"

Ethan smiled and then relaxed. This he knew how to address.

"Lydia, you do know that I find you attractive, smart, and you stimulate my mind and my imagination, right?"

She reached out and placed her hand over his mouth.

"You can't say that. Oh, my goodness, we really can't date."

He took her hand from his mouth and kissed the inside of her wrist.

"I can say that because it's the truth. Now if you say to me you don't want to date me, I can accept that. It's always a woman's right to say no. I'd be curious as to why. Do you find me unattractive?"

"No," she whispered.

"I took a bath today, but maybe you don't like my soap or cologne."

He saw her trying to hide her smile.

"No, I don't have any issue with your personal hygiene."

"I would be surprised, but I have to ask if maybe it's my background that offends you?"

"Not at all. I think I may even be liking some of your ways."

"Then that means what you're really saying is that you're scared."

He looked into her brown eyes, and she blinked and broke his gaze.

"You're right. I'm scared, Ethan. You are a lot for a woman to take on. You're attractive, rich, and you seem like a nice guy."

"I don't get it. I thought I'd be a catch."

Lydia smiled sadly. "I'm not like other women."

"I've looked Lydia you are more than you think you. You're a gem in disguise that everyone can see but you."

She smiled and shook her head. "I have baggage, Ethan."

He touched her cheek. "It's a good thing. That way we can get matching baggage. I don't need you to change, Lydia. I like the woman you are."

She nibbled on her lower lip and then took a deep breath. "Well, if you're sure, pass that box!"

He laughed and pulled the box out. "This box?" He handed it over to her, and she held it to her chest.

"Well, come in and bring your stuff. You're making a scene out here for my neighbors."

She walked him in through the front door. He made two trips, but he finally brought everything into the house. She showed him the kitchen and took a seat at the small table. As he spread out to cook, she went ahead and opened the golden box.

"Mana must have tasted like this." She grabbed another chocolate and took a small bite into the confection. Her eyes slowly closed as she savored the morsel.

Ethan had to stop setting up to look at her. She was the personification of female sex appeal. It was one of the many things that attracted him to her. She was always upfront. The men of Sweet Blooms had overlooked this treasure.

He started to prepare dinner by laying out all of the ingredients and setting up the pots. "So, dinner is going to be chicken francese with pasta," he said as he continued to unpack. "What kind of pasta would you like? I brought two—spaghetti and fettuccini."

"I can't even pronounce what you just said, so I'll leave it to you."

"Wow, if I thought I could get that response from you all the time, I'd buy you more chocolate."

"It's just because it's late in the day and my faculties are being dulled by pleasure."

"So, let's talk about other important matters. Now that we're dating."

Lydia choked and had to go to the sink to get water. "You did that just get me to stop eating my chocolate."

"I think people talk about dating all the time. I heard there's a pattern. It goes something like dating and then relationship."

"Men do not talk about relationships. They talk about how we need to explore our feelings while we see other people. Just so we can make sure that we aren't rushing into anything."

Ethan had stopped working in the kitchen, and he was looking at her.

Lydia looked a bit sheepish. "I'm sorry. I guess that was my baggage showing up."

Ethan picked up the conversation as he filleted the chicken cutlets and set the saucepan on the stove.

"No worries. My baggage has women talking about money more than relationships."

"Ouch, sorry."

Ethan kept on putting stock in the pot as he waved off her comment. "Don't be sorry. I said that to let you know that we both have some baggage, and it's not limited to you."

"You sure do like to talk a lot," Lydia said.

Ethan laughed. "I would think that would be a plus, counselor."

Lydia waved him off. "Please, I hear people talk all day. In my private life, I'm not so talky at all."

Ethan finished up the meal and set the table.

After Lydia took the first bite, her eyes popped open. "This is really good."

"You sound surprised."

Lydia dug in with her fork. "Let's just say that I've had some experience with people cooking for me, and I was totally prepared to endure tonight."

"I'm glad I didn't disappoint."

Lydia looked at him. "You don't disappoint at all, Ethan." The night continued, and when they were done, Ethan pulled out his iPad and turned on some music.

"What are you doing?"

"I figured, I fed you, and we've rested a bit and now we can end the night with a little dancing."

He could see she was unsure, but when he extended his hand, she slowly put hers in his. He led her into the middle of her living room and then pulled her in close to him. She stopped when there was about a foot between them.

"I want you closer, Lydia," he said quietly. He could see the rise and fall of her chest. He didn't rush her. When she finally made the last steps into his arms, he let out a sigh and wrapped his hands around her waist.

"I was a little nervous you were going to leave me hanging, and I thought I'd have to break out the Nutella."

He kept his hands on her waist, guiding her to the music. He took in the smell of her hair and felt how warm she was to the touch. How she fit in his arms like a missing puzzle piece. With her arms on his shoulders, he was able to look into her face.

"We can stop dancing, Lydia."

She looked up, and he could see anxiety in her gaze. He dropped his hands, and she held them to her hips.

"It's not you. I can't dance, and I'm stressing that I'll step on your foot and do some permanent damage. I mean, I don't have small feet, so if they come down on you, you are definitely going to feel it."

He smiled at her and spoke slowly.

"I think the best way to handle this is for you to put your hands somewhere you feel comfortable, and I'll go ahead and lead again. I need you to look at me, not our feet. It's easier that way."

She looked at him as if he had lost his mind. "You know that makes no sense. I'm doing this for you."

"I think you need help."

"That's what I've been telling you!"

He leaned down and kissed her. He never stopped moving with the music. He could feel her hands tighten on his shoulders as he moved from her mouth and continued to kiss her lightly across her cheek and down her neck. When he made it to the crook of her neck, he inhaled deeply and then continued back to her earlobe.

When he came back to her mouth, he kissed her a little longer and then he pulled back. "Lydia," he whispered, hovering above her lips.

She didn't say a word. Her eyes were closed, and her lips parted as if they were inviting him again for another kiss. She was woman personified, and again he had that moment when being with her was more than right; it was something he had been waiting for. He was about to kiss her again when the doorbell rang.

Lydia's eyes popped open and then her head fell to his chest. "Who could have such horrible timing?" she said into his chest.

He followed her to the door. She looked out of the peephole and then turned around, plastering her body to the door as if she wanted to hold it closed. The doorbell rang again.

Ethan was confused as to why she wouldn't answer the door.

"Don't you think you should get that?"

She placed a finger on his lips and mouthed, "It's my mother."

The doorbell rang again. "Lydia, please, are you home?"

Lydia's head fell onto her chest. Ethan grinned and mouthed to her, "Do the right thing."

Lydia took a big breath.

"Coming."

Ethan went to the kitchen pack up, and Lydia opened the door.

"Mother."

"Lydia, I—" Mara looked through the kitchen opening and saw Ethan. "Oh, I didn't know you had company."

"No, it's not a problem. Come in."

Mara hesitated and then stood firm. "No, no, I won't interfere. I'll see you tomorrow."

"Are you sure?"

"Yes, have a good dinner."

When the door closed, Ethan came out and leaned against the doorway.

"That is the first time I've ever been caught by a mother."

"Oh, my goodness, do you know what that means?"

Ethan shook his head.

"It means my mom knows we're together."

"And?"

"It's big."

"I'm not sure I get the gravity of the situation, but I have another golden box and some Nutella to help you tell the story."

Lydia nodded her head. "It might help me with explaining. Where did you say the box was?"

Nine

Ethan looked at his father sitting across from him and knew nothing that he wanted would come from this. It wasn't often that he let anything personal interfere with his business, but this was one of those time he was at a crossroads.

He looked at the resume in front of him and tried to vet it for any obvious reasons for him to say no, but he didn't see any, and that was just making the situation worse. He knew his father was looking at him and waiting for him to make a decision.

"Why did you bring me this resume, dad?" Ethan asked as he looked at it again.

"She's someone in town who has a degree. She's an outskirter, Ethan. She won't have any connections to get a job in town. I saw you with the mayor's girl, and I figured one of you would have a position for her."

"I take it you know about me and the deed here in Sweet Blooms."

"I totally understand it now because the mayor had to explain it to me. I wish my son could have explained it to me first."

Ethan knew he hadn't fully explained why he was

back in town. He had some reservations about everyone, and experience had told him to wait and see how people reacted to him being there.

"I did some looking into things. Penny is a good fit for you and your business stuff. I think she will be easier to work with and you'd be helping out your own people. Giving back is what they call it, right?"

"Dad, I don't need to hire a friend or someone who will look good when it's time to do some type of public relations. I need to hire someone who understands real estate terms and basic business issues. I have people I work with back in the city, but I'm going to be busy since Adam Cade agreed to do some work here. That means I need someone to take care of babysitting whatever I assign them when it comes to the deeds in Sweet Booms."

"I think it's really smart of you to know you can't be everywhere," Barrick said. "I think you should consider that Penny is someone who knows the town and the people. You could hire someone with that book knowledge, but they wouldn't know Sweet Blooms."

Ethan nodded, looking again at the resume. "I don't want to tell you if it's going to be her or not. I can tell you that she is one of the two people that I have decided to choose between."

"Can you tell me what the other is like? If you do, maybe I'll say that it doesn't make sense to even consider her."

"Rafael is a project manager like no other. He's got a lot of experience in different fields, and he knows real estate law. He's gone to different people and looked at deals, not just from a financial point of view. What he specializes in is doing what's right for everyone involved.

Having buy-in with the place you are going to work at is important."

"Well, I can tell you about Penny. She doesn't have as much experience as your guy, but she knows Sweet Blooms. She has a real estate degree, and she has an easy-going nature. She loves the town and will work hard. She also has a business degree."

Ethan shuffled through the papers on his desk.

"I checked her references, and everyone said she is a real go-getter. They said she's thorough, and their all-around report was she was a good candidate."

If it had been anything else, Ethan realized he wouldn't hesitate, but this was so important to him and to his future. Lydia had taught him to be honest. He didn't want to mess this up in his town.

Barrick cleared his throat. "You know you have two good candidates. What is the worse that could happen, Ethan? If you pick the wrong one, you can just go back and get the other one. Look, you need to do what's best for you and your company. I just brought her to the table because I thought you could help. You do what's best for you."

With those words, Barrick left Ethan alone in the office. He knew things were about to change. He could always tell when a shift in a deal was coming. He wouldn't have time to address this later; he had to do it now.

He looked at the paper again. His first thought was to go with Rafael, but he didn't want to be narrow-minded. He needed someone who understood small town politics on day one. He picked up his cell and called Larisa.

Mara had finally made it to the Cade ranch. She wasn't really sure how to get there as she had never been invited, but now that she was here, she could see why they were going to build on it. It was beautiful.

"Mayor?"

She turned at the sound of her title and saw Ethan Young standing on the porch.

"You chose a beautiful place to meet," she said.

Ethan smiled. "It wasn't really up to me. I'm working here, and the land is beautiful. As you can see, the house still needs work. I think the only thing still working with the house is this porch." He stepped off the porch and led the way to a nearby shed.

"Please, come inside," he said as he gestured for her to come in.

Mara knew after talking with Barrick and seeing Ethan having dinner at Lydia's place that it was time to resolve the issue with Ethan. She still needed to address the issues with Lydia, but she could at least get her mayoral duties out of the way. Inside there were pictures of mock-ups of what the town would look like after all the renovations and rebuilding had been done.

"I only have instant coffee and water," Ethan said as he took a seat at the desk. Mara shook her head. She couldn't eat or drink anything today.

"No, thank you. I'm fine," Mara replied. When Mara thought on this last night, it seemed like it was the best idea. Now that she was here, she had to admit that it wasn't as clean as she thought it would be. Looking at Ethan, she could see the appeal he held for Lydia. In truth, she knew she should be happy for both of them.

They had such passion and idealism.

"I won't waste your time. I wanted to talk to you about Sweet Blooms. Are you open to a conversation?" Mara asked.

"I'm not sure, Mayor. It all depends on what exactly you're proposing," he said as he took a drink of his coffee.

"I'm willing to pay for the deeds," Mara blurted out.

"I don't know if you have enough to buy them, and I'm not sure I want to let go of such a valuable investment."

"Is this spite, Mr. Young?"

"Spite?"

"Are you trying to make the town pay, and humble them by letting them know you own Sweet Blooms?"

Ethan smiled. "I can see where Lydia gets her directness. The short answer is no. I wasn't sure that I could say that when I first arrived, but I can now. I'm not interested in making the town pay. I am interested in keeping an asset that could be worth more in the future and possibly giving dividends. So, here is my proposal to you.

"The plan I have for Sweet Blooms is for it to be fully remodeled. It will keep its charm because it's so valuable to city people. I see we can redo the community center, and we can make some stores provide training to our kids. I've talked about it with Adam Cade, and he's completely on board with it. I won't sell my deed until the town is finished."

Mara heard him, and she pressed her lips together. It was the only way she could hold back her comments. What he planned had been large, bold, and beyond anything she had ever imagined.

"It could be decades before all that is done. I know you may be a man of integrity, but things happen. You could have children and pass it on to them, and they'll sell the place to others. We as a town need more security than that." She fidgeted a moment in her chair. "How about this? You make it a clause that we have to have the first option on the sale of the deeds. If we provide a reasonable offer, then you will give us the land, and the town won't have to enter any bidding with any other buyer, and we will have exclusive first buy rights."

Mara waited to see what Ethan would do. The terms were bold on both sides, and she wasn't even sure that Sweet Blooms would be able to compete with a "reasonable offer" or that he would be able to finish all the building he mentioned. But she knew if she didn't do something, her town would constantly be in danger. Better to make a deal with the devil you knew rather than the one you didn't.

"Done," Ethan said with a smile.

Mara saw that smile, and she laughed at herself.

"Well played, Ethan. I'm curious. If I had said we couldn't wait, what would you have taken?"

"I would have given it in trust for free."

Mara shook her head. "Yet you let me negotiate for nothing."

"Oh, I don't know. I'm feeling way richer now than when we started this conversation."

Mara laughed and shook her head. It was another reason she could see that Lydia would appreciate a man who understood the business, had a sense of wit, and also had a moral direction about things that were important.

"Are we done, Mayor?" Ethan asked.

Mara smiled at Ethan and nodded. "Yes, we are. I'll be looking for the paperwork."

"Of course. I'll have my new assistant send it. Her name is Penny Stewart." Mara nodded and left the ranch. As she was leaving, she thought about the fact that Ethan had a new assistant. She also thought about what Barrick had said about how he thought only another outskirter would be good enough for his son.

Mara knew Penny Stewart. She was a recent graduate who had returned to Sweet Blooms.

"I don't feel like you're taking me to dinner," teased Ethan. Lydia looked back at him and rolled her eyes. She hadn't given him much warning, just that he should meet her at her job. When he arrived, instead of her being dressed in a suit, she was dressed in jeans.

They arrived at the community center and went into the basement where the offices were. Then she turned to him and sat him down.

"I know I didn't give you a lot of warning about coming here tonight."

"No, you didn't."

"But I wanted you to see the work we do. Tonight, is young men's night. They come here once a week and we all talk. It's a program that was set up by Joshua Case. He works at the school. He's actually the school guidance counselor, and he wanted the guys to have a place to go."

Ethan could see that Lydia was rambling as she spoke. Her breathing had picked up a bit, and she was nibbling on her lower lip again.

"It seems odd you're here if it's a guy group," he commented, eyeing her a bit suspiciously. Lydia actually blushed.

"Joshua is out tonight, and the guys have let me sit in before. I've been working with some of them individually when they have questions that they would like to ask a girl but aren't sure about. It's been one growth session after another for me."

Ethan waited for the other part to be said. He knew Lydia by now, and if she could help someone, she would. Even if helping someone meant she would have to impose on someone else, like him.

"You want me to do something, Lydia, but what?"

"I don't want you to think you have to do anything," she said with her hands held up.

He grabbed both of her hands and then brought them to his lips.

"I'm here. Let's see what's going on."

Her face lit up as if it were Christmas. "Okay, let's go."

When they entered the room, he could see there was a table in the back of the room, and it had food and drink on it. There was a total of three guys in the room, ranging from the ages of thirteen to nineteen. All of them were outskirter boys. When they saw him, they all tapped each other and formed a group as if they could protect each other.

He remembered being this age. He stepped back and waited. When Lydia came into the room, they all smiled. She went to each boy individually and hugged each one. She asked them questions, and then she turned to introduce him.

"Guys, Joshua couldn't be here tonight. But I have

someone who I thought you might want to meet. His name is Ethan Young. You know how I told you sometimes I might bring guests? Well, he's one."

The guys looked him over, and the oldest one, named Tim, stepped towards him.

"So, what are you here to talk about?"

Ethan gave the boy a stare and then stepped into the classroom.

"I'm here to talk about how you can make your life better and leave Sweet Blooms."

Lydia's mouth opened in shock, but all of the boys laughed.

"If you think there is a way to get out of Sweet Blooms, that means you haven't seen all of it. We're from the—"

"You're from the outskirts. I know; I'm from there too," Ethan said.

The boys were all silent, and then the smallest looked to Lydia.

She nodded to confirm his story. "It's true. He's from Sweet Blooms. His father is Barrick Young."

"The bull man!" The youngest clapped his hands over his mouth and looked at Ethan as if he expected him to get upset or to have some sort of reaction.

Ethan raised his hand and had to smile. How many times, when he was younger, would he joke with his friends about how his dad was built so solid that there wasn't anything he couldn't wrestle to the ground.

"It's fine, and yes, that would be my dad."

Tim came closer and looked at Ethan before going back to his seat.

"So, you're going to tell us how you got out of Sweet Blooms?" Tim asked.

Lydia sat with the boys and looked at him. They were all waiting with bated breath.

"I don't think this story is going to be as exciting as you all think it will be."

Lydia jumped in. "We won't know unless you tell it," she said with a smile.

"Well, the first thing you need to have is a plan. Nothing works without a plan. I had a plan that I would leave after I graduated from high school, and that's what I did."

One of the boys moaned. "If the plan doesn't start until I graduate high school then I'm never going to leave."

Lydia looked over. "Gary, why do you say that?"

"Ms. M, I don't do well in math at all. I've taken the class twice now, and I'm no better than when I started it."

Ethan saw Gary and sympathized. "Listen up. How many of you have problems in school?" Ethan asked.

All of the boys raised their hands.

"This is what I'll do. Why don't we take some time, and I'll meet with each one of you? We can work on making a plan for you so you can get an idea of what it looks like. As for the class problems, I'll get you a tutor to help you out."

The boys said thank you, and the look of happiness on Lydia's face was priceless. The night went by quickly, and before long it was time to go home. When Lydia dropped him off at the courthouse so he could get his truck, he stopped her before she pulled away.

"Yes?"

"I wanted to say thank you."

Lydia smiled at him and looked confused. He reached out and traced her cheek.

"I always wanted to do something, but there never seemed to be anything for me. I don't remember those kinds of programs when I was growing up."

Leaning into his hand, she sighed. "There probably weren't any of those programs when you were growing up. But you give me hope, Ethan. You didn't have any of those and you turned out pretty okay. I'm hoping that, with these programs, they'll find their way as well."

He watched her drive away, and he knew. If he was unsure, it was settled. Lydia Mason was the one for him.

Ten

"You should have seen him," Lydia said as Yolanda opened up the boxes of take-out and placed them on the tables. The aroma of Chinese food filled the air.

"He talked to them, and he was so sincere, and the kids could tell he was sincere too. I know Joshua is amazing, but he had such a connection with them."

Yolanda took out the utensils and the plates and put them in front of Lydia. When she started to serve out the food, for every spoonful she put on Lydia's plate, she put two on hers.

"What are you doing?" Lydia asked with a smile. "I mean, if you're hungry, I guess—"

When Yolanda looked shocked, Lydia pointed at her plate. "Is there something you wanted to tell me?"

"Oh, you are talking about my plate size. Well, I have to have that much food, so I have enough energy to listen to how good and great Ethan Young is," she said, laughing.

Lydia waved her off and then went to get the water bottles.

"I hear you. I'll try to curtail my story."

Yolanda sat across from Lydia and began eating her lunch. "It doesn't bother me that you are deciding to go full Ethan. In some ways, I think it's the best thing you could do. Like I said before, if you're going to fall for a guy, make sure that he looks good and he's well off. I have to say, Ethan Young fits both of the criteria."

Lydia took a couple of bites of food and then looked at Yolanda.

"You don't approve of how much I stand up for him," she said in as much of a neutral tone as she could manage.

Yolanda put down her food and reached out to Lydia. Lydia looked at her friend's hand across the table and then looked back into Yolanda's eyes.

"I spoke so highly of him because I didn't think he would. Because I had mistakenly judged him to be one way and it turned out that he wasn't like that at all. I wanted to right his name to a person who really mattered to me."

"I think what he did and how he did it says a lot about him. The thing is, he's not my friend—you are. I'm worried because I'm not hearing the other parts that should go with this show. Such as what is the relationship between you and Mr. Wonderful?"

Lydia sighed and sat back in her chair. "He says that we're dating."

Yolanda leaned back and started eating but didn't say a word.

"You can't do that! You can't get me to confess and then leave me out there with no judgment"

Pointing her fork at Lydia, she began. "First of all, I can do that. Second of all, what do you expect me to say when I ask you about your relationship and you say, 'He says we're dating.' Really, Lydia? It's time to put on the big girl undies and do the one thing you hate to do. The big C-word."

"Okay, we're friends who are dating."

"Are you two doing the do?"

"No! I said we're dating friends. I don't do friends with benefits!"

Yolanda held up a hand in defense.

"Listen, it's an occupational hazard for me to ask all these questions. You'd be amazed how many cases are lost just because the lawyer never asked their client if they were guilty or not."

"I hear you, I hear you."

Yolanda knocked on the top of the desk. "I want to make sure you really do hear me. Ethan Young is fully grown. He's not some young boy or even some college guy who wants to find an easy way to get ahead."

"I know he's a grown man. I get it."

"Lydia, I want you to be happy, and if Ethan makes you happy, I'm all for him. Even if he doesn't turn out to be Mister Right, I'm still for him because you deserve some happiness."

Lydia looked at her friend and thought about Ethan.

"He makes me happy. He shows me things I've never seen before, and no matter what happens, I won't regret this."

Yolanda patted her on the hand and then kept moving. Lydia had no illusions about what was going on. Yolanda thought she would get too emotionally involved with Ethan. It was too late for that. She was sure she was well past the safe point. She wasn't sure what would happen. No one could be, but what she was sure about was for once she was going to grab on and hold on, and see where it landed.

Whatever happened between her and Ethan would be just fine with her.

Mara rang the bell knowing Lydia may not be home today. Really, who was she kidding? If Lydia saw her out here, she might just ignore her. Mara had become the mayor of Sweet Blooms with no husband. She knew about patience, perseverance, and having goals.

Her life hadn't been easy, and she was happy that it hadn't. She wasn't expecting Lydia to give her a pass because of what she had been through, but she wanted at least the ability to start off from scratch with her. Mara wasn't ready to give up on having any kind of healthy relationship with Lydia.

After talking with Charlie, she was willing to admit she had some flaws, but giving up on things that mattered to her wasn't one of them. She rang the doorbell again and, finally, she heard someone moving.

"I'm here, and I'm awake," Lydia said. "I was almost done with a brief."

"I wasn't sure. For a moment I thought you were just trying to outwait me."

Mara saw Lydia's head shake and her hand rub her forehead. She didn't say it wasn't true. Mara stepped aside.

"I'm surprised no appointment was sent to me," Lydia said.

"I have a secretary. Why are you so upset when I use her for the thing she is being paid to do?"

"Maybe because I'm your daughter," she mumbled.

Lydia closed the door and went into her living room

and plopped down on the sofa. Mara took in the house. She didn't know what she expected inside the house, but the outside of the house was an homage to silliness and fairytales.

"I think the inside of the house suits you better," she said. "I don't know what happened to the outside, but maybe you can get the inside guy to do the outside for you."

Mara looked at Lydia sitting in her oversized tee shirt and ripped faded jeans. Her hair was in a sloppy ponytail, and her face was bare as usual. She saw Lydia trying to find the words she wanted to say. She expected to hear a thank you for making the observation and offering a solution.

"I'm curious, mother, you came all this way to pick apart what you didn't like in my life?"

"No." Mara sat back and tried to think of something else to say. Although, if she were honest, she couldn't understand why Lydia was offended at all. She thought about the words she had said, the tone, and how factual they were.

Mara looked at Lydia, and she was so proud of her. She didn't know what to say, but what she did know was that every day she looked at Lydia, it was a miracle. She saw Lydia with so many good qualities, and she was such a good person at heart. It was painful to see her so free with everyone in town but then avoided her like a pariah. She must have been quiet a bit too long because Lydia looked concerned when she spoke.

"Are you okay?" Lydia asked.

Clearing her throat, she pasted on a smile and replied. "I'm fine, really. I was just looking at you and thinking. I'm so proud of you."

Lydia looked shocked. "Thank you."

"I thought it was time that we had a talk."

"We talk almost every day."

"Lydia, please. I don't mean like that. I mean it's time we talked as if we are family."

"Oh, those type of talks. I'm not really fond of those. Whenever we do those, it sounds like a conversation that goes over what's wrong with me or what I am doing wrong."

Mara looked at her daughter's annoyed face and swallowed down that moment of weakness that threatened to overcome her. She hadn't realized until that moment how far apart they had become.

"I know that I may not show it all the time, or at all if your response is the gauge. But I do love you. I would like for us to be more than just work companions if that is even possible."

Lydia moved to the edge of the sofa and looked at her mother.

"Are you telling me you came here to work on our non-existent mother-daughter relationship?"

Mara took a big breath and let it out before nodding.

"Well, that calls for coffee and chocolate. Would you like some?"

Mara was a bit confused, but she said yes.

"I feel better when my hands are moving, and I happen to love chocolate and coffee. So, I have to ask, what brought on this motherly care?"

"You make it sound like I never cared. The truth is, I've always cared about you, but I have to say that recently, with your interactions with that Ethan boy, I've been more concerned that maybe I didn't prep you to deal with men like that."

"You know, it's funny to me that you are concerned about Ethan, yet you weren't concerned about any other person I brought home."

Mara snorted. "You can hardly blame me for the last fellow. I told you he was bad for you the first time I met him."

"You didn't give me a reason either."

"I'm your mother. Isn't my word enough? It's funny to me that the town can listen to what I say, and they don't ask me for the truth in triplicate. My own daughter, though, needs proof before she will even consider listening to me."

Lydia set the cups on the table, and next to each cup she put down two gold pieces of chocolate. They ate in silence, and as Mara was finishing off the last bit of chocolate, she had to speak. "If only your life choices were as good as this chocolate."

"Okay, I'm done."

"Done?"

"Mother, every time we get together, we are snapping and judging each other. I don't know if we can have a regular relationship because I can't take you criticizing me all the time. I am touched that you thought I would need a mother now, but I assure you, I can handle Ethan. Whatever else I decide to do, I will make sure that it doesn't reflect poorly on you. Now, if you'll excuse me, I really do need to get back to that brief."

Mara nodded. She stood up and looked at Lydia. She wasn't sure what to say so she fell back on what she knew. "I hope you have a productive day." With that, she left. She hadn't made it past the last fairy when her vision started to blur. She'd try again, but today…today she was just hurting.

Eleven

"My mother doesn't get any easier the older I get," Lydia said as she dug her fork into the spaghetti and meatballs Ethan had made for them. "She decided she just wanted to be my mother again."

Ethan looked at Lydia and saw how worked up she was. He had said he wanted to come over tonight to cook and they had just moved from the kitchen to the small dining room table.

"Well, I think it's a huge improvement. Not so long ago we were both on the other side of the door, and you were wondering if you should open the door. Now we're talking about how she wants to start a relationship. Do you want a relationship with her?" he asked.

"Of course! I don't know. I want to be with her, but every time we're together, she goes and criticizes me. She picked on my house. I feel like there is nothing that I'm going to do that will ever live up to her standards. If it's wrong, I do it. I'm a constant reminder of who she was and what happens when you don't plan."

"Then she must be jealous to see what it looks like to live free."

Lydia smiled. "Oh, I'm the lawyer, but that was

good. I'm thinking you might have a brain in that gorgeous head."

"I'm glad you've admitted to your addiction to me. Admitting is the first step."

Lydia waved him off. "I wish she would leave me alone and just go back to our status quo."

"I hear you, but sometimes there's a reason why people change."

Lydia ate some more of the spaghetti, slurped up her noodles, and then swallowed.

"I hear you. She told me that she wanted a relationship. I see she's getting older. But no matter what else is changing in her life, she still maintains her ability to criticize anything and everything. Or I should say she always maintains the ability to criticize me."

Ethan put some garlic bread on her plate. "It's hard with parents. You want to be there for her, but you want her to change to make it easier. People are complicated."

She stopped eating and looked at Ethan. "You're really good about seeing all sides. I'm feeling beyond guilty because I want it to just be over. I want her to go back to being the mayor and not my mother."

"Does it look like it's going that way?"

"No," she said as she let out a deep sigh. "Okay, that's enough of me hemming and hawing about family. Why don't we talk about something new? Tell me how your day went."

Ethan smiled. "Well, this week has been interesting. My life has been enriched since I started dating this amazing woman."

Lydia laughed. "Okay, besides your good fortune to be dating this amazing woman, how's work?"

"I'm doing some negotiations while I'm here, and I wanted to have someone assist me who would be permanent. I wanted to make sure I hired the right person, and I had two options."

"You must do this all the time. Why was this time any different?"

"I had two options. One was a person who had experience but didn't have small town experience, and the person who has small town experience, that was all they had."

"Okay, so who did you choose?"

"I picked the small-town experience only, thinking it was more important to have small town hitting the ground."

"I'm still not understanding. It seems like this was a good decision."

"The person I chose came from a personal reference, like a friend. That's not my norm, and the other thing is, I didn't feel settled with the decision."

Lydia waved her fork in the air. "I'm a big proponent of following your gut. If you feel like it wasn't something you were comfortable with, I'd go with the decision that lets you sleep at night."

"We'll see because I've already hired the newbie. I'll see how it goes."

The conversation lagged while they finished up dinner and then Lydia cleared her throat.

"I wanted to ask a question that we never discussed."

"It must be serious."

"Why do you say that?"

"You sat up, and you've cleared your throat. You have a couple of tells that say this is about to become a serious conversation."

"Well, I know we said we were dating, but we never clarified if you wanted to date other people while we were together."

He stood up and pulled her to him. He looked directly into her eyes and then tucked her hair behind her ears.

"I'm dating you, and that means that I'm committed to you. I'm not looking around for the right one. If I say to you let's date, it means I think you are the right one and I want you to come around to my way of thinking that I'm the right person for you. I'm not looking for anyone else. I'm not hoping for a new one."

She closed her eyes and leaned towards him. He pulled her closer and cupped her face in his hands and kissed her. "Are you telling me you would like to date others?"

"No, but we got here in a weird way, and I didn't want you to feel trapped."

Ethan smiled. "Please feel free to trap me anytime you'd like."

The next morning, Lydia was greeted at her front door by Ethan. He had a large coffee and a small, gold box of chocolate. She was pleasantly surprised and eager to get to the chocolate, but the man once again surprised her.

"Are you here because you like me or because you're really taken by the décor on the front step?"

Ethan looked around. "I have to admit it's a unique experience walking to the door and realizing there are so many eyes on me, but rest assured, I came to have your eyes on me."

"Sure you did."

She thought he would hand her the chocolate or the coffee, but instead, he leaned in and kissed her. The kiss was quick, unexpected, and a great way to start the day. Not wanting to look like a total dweeb in the doorway, she reached for the coffee and led him into the kitchen.

Ethan set up the coffee. "Oh, I can see it now. Every time I come over, we wind up in the kitchen. Next thing I know, you'll have me trapped in here."

Lydia laughed. "Well, you are the better cook, and I believe in people expressing themselves.

"I didn't come to make breakfast. I came to drop you off at work."

Lydia put her hands on her cheeks and said, "Oh, NO!"

Ethan laughed and shook his head. "Hurry up. I'll drop you off, and I thought I'd pick you up and bring you out to the Cade ranch."

"I thought they were still working on it," she said.

"They are, but there's a temp building built on it, and the grounds are ready. Adam just needs to fix the house. It's got good bones, but that's it."

"Okay, it's a date," Lydia said.

Ethan clapped. "I'm glad you're getting the hang of saying that."

Just as he promised, he showed up later for lunch. They drove out to the Cade ranch and found a picnic table. When she asked him about it, Ethan said he had brought several of them out for the people to eat on instead of sitting on the ground.

When he brought her to the table, he had already laid out everything for them. She took a bite of one of the sandwich triangles and then looked around.

Ethan put his hand up. "Just stop right there. I will not apologize for my organization when it comes to food. I like to eat."

Lydia smiled. "I'm going to be the last person to complain about anything that touches my food. The expression makes so much sense to me now. The way to a man's heart is through his stomach."

"Is that where I'm getting, Lydia?"

She looked at him and swallowed. "Please, I can imagine that I'm not the type of woman you've dated before."

Ethan raised an eyebrow. "And what kind of woman would that be?"

Lydia framed her face with her hands and batted her eyelashes. "I think you went out with those skinny Minnie girls. The ones who look great on the cover of a magazine but who don't do a lot of eating. I can see that must have been very upsetting to you considering how much you like to cook."

He couldn't stop laughing. "Is this your idea of table talk?"

"Well, I'm just pointing out what I think is pretty obvious to everyone."

"Yes, it was your all-knowingness that really attracted me to you in the beginning."

Lydia sniffed. "I would like to toss the sandwich at you, but my hunger prevents me."

She looked around and realized Ethan was right; the Cade ranch was beautiful. The house was in shambles, but the green lawn next to the mini pond was straight from a postcard. She was throwing herself into the moment, and Ethan didn't disappoint. Being with

Ethan was easy and brought her a new kind of comfort and outlet of expression. He was smart in a way that intrigued her. He shared some of the things they both knew about Sweet Blooms. He was funny and sexy all in the same package. It seemed like she had finally gotten it right.

"Ethan," a deep barrel voice called out.

Lydia's head popped up when she heard that voice. She wasn't sure if she should run or throw her body over Ethan's to protect him. She knew who it was. But a person just didn't get used to seeing Barrick. Yes, it was Barrick Young.

Barrick was dressed in overalls, and he was looking at them as if they should be ashamed of themselves.

"Hello, Mr. Young.", Lydia said.

Ethan didn't move. Lydia instead saw him cock his head to the side and then he spoke. "Dad?"

Barrick gave Ethan a momentary look, and then he shifted his gaze back to Lydia.

"You're the mayor's girl? I saw you at the pond with Ethan a bit back."

"Yes, I am. Please forgive me for not introducing myself earlier. I'm Lydia Mason."

He shook her hand and then Barrick looked at Ethan.

"I came by to thank you for what you done for Penny."

Lydia looked at Ethan. What had he done for Penny? Who was Penny?

Ethan waved it off. "She'll either do well at the job or she won't."

Lydia listened to what they were saying. Now the conversation about the person Ethan was supposed to hire and how he was having feelings about it was becoming all too clear.

Barrick turned to Lydia. "My boy is a bit close-mouthed. He was kind enough to help one of our own to get a job. Penny has just graduated, and Ethan knows how hard it can be for us to get a break."

Lydia smiled. "I think it's hard for all graduates to find a job."

Barrick smiled. "Maybe, but you seemed to have done well with finding a job at the courthouse. We don't have those kinds of connections. Ethan understands that."

Lydia kept her smile in place. "It's funny how people remember who they are and where they come from when they need something. I believe in helping people, but if we're going to use Ethan as an example, then I can't imagine why Penny would need help."

Barrick turned to Ethan. "How do you think this is going to work? Where do you think this is going?"

Lydia went stock still, and she had to remember to breathe. This was the million-dollar question, wasn't it? She knew Ethan, and she had talked about dating, and he had talked about moving on in the relationship, but it was a different issue altogether to vocalize that intent to someone else. She wouldn't hold it against him if he couldn't do it.

"I know what I'm doing here. I'm building something with someone who I think is very special. I'm hoping she'll have me."

Barrick looked between both of them and then laughed. "You know how crazy this is? It never works!"

Ethan shook his head and spoke in a low voice. "Just because it didn't work for you doesn't mean it won't work for anyone ever again."

Lydia watched the play between then like a tennis match. She couldn't interject, and she couldn't walk away. When it was clear that Ethan wasn't going to back down, Barrick looked at them both and shook his head.

"How long do you think she'll want to slum around with you?"

Ethan held out his hand. "Stop. You don't know Lydia. She's amazing, giving, and the most open-hearted person I know. I'm sure we'll have problems, but whatever they are, we'll work on it."

Barrick looked at Ethan. "Well, it looks like you have him totally convinced. When you get tired of him, try to leave him some dignity." With that, Barrick left them alone.

"I'm sorry. I didn't want to be a burden between you and your dad," she said.

"It was the truth."

She didn't know quite what to say. "You know, you tell me about my mom, so let me tell you that the problem with your dad is that he's lonely."

Ethan stopped eating and looked at her.

"The problem is, I know you're right, but he won't let me be around him unless it's all his rules. It's the reason I left home. I don't know if there's anything we can do about it now."

Lydia reached out to him. "Don't say that."

Ethan gave her a sad smile. "I know no one likes to say those things, but the truth of it is, at some point we need to let people be."

"Well, besides not wanting anyone to be alone, I definitely don't want your dad to have to know what it's like to be alone. Being the mayor's kid didn't make me popular in a good way. People would ask if they could get drugs or do other things and if my mom would look the other way. Some of them invited me to illegal parties with the thought I'd stay, but I didn't. Instead, I had to go back and tell my mom what had happened.

"It didn't earn me any friends at school, and my mom would always blame my impulsive, passive nature. If only I wasn't so curious, I wouldn't get into trouble. When I ran into my last boyfriend who wanted the riches, he thought my mom had instead of me, she told me that was an example of what poor planning and impulsiveness got you."

Ethan got up, walked around the table, and went to sit next to Lydia. He brought both of her hands to his lips. His grip tightened when she tried to pull away.

"Beautiful, look at me," he whispered.

Lydia didn't have a choice. When was the last time a man had called her beautiful?

"Lydia, you're amazing," he told her. "It's that inquisitive nature that helps to find people in need. It's that impulsiveness that says you can help others and fix things we all overlook. It's true, not everyone will be honest. Not everyone will even tell the truth. What's important is that you aren't alone. Ask anyone—the boys at the meet, or even Yolanda."

Lydia nibbled on her lower lip. "I'm proud of my accomplishments," she said. "I don't regret anything, and I think that's one of my biggest accomplishments. Look, our parents have something in common. The both of them are stubborn in their own way."

Ethan laughed. "You want to trade?"

Lydia picked up Ethan's hands and brought them to

her lips. "He made an effort to come. That's got to say something for him."

"Yes, it does. The problem is, I don't think it says anything positive for him, though. My dad and I have old issues we may never be able to resolve. I think there is more leeway for you and your mother."

"You might just be really optimistic."

Ethan leaned in and kissed her on the side of her mouth. "My Lydia is bold, passionate, and smart. I'm sure you've got this."

Lydia smiled and held on to every word. He had just called her his. Then the words from Yolanda come back to her as if they were ghosts. And Lydia pushed them away. This was worth all the risks she had talked about before. Ethan was worth the risk. This wasn't about sex, or desperation, or even fear of being alone. This was about the two of them.

"I'm not sure I've got this, but I'll definitely give it a try before I consider getting a ticket and going to visit Katmandu," she told him. He gave her a stern look, and she shrugged. "I'm working on it, just in my own way."

Twelve

Ethan's words had gotten through. Here she was reaching out to her mother. When Lydia thought about how Barrick and Ethan were, she was more than happy with the situation. She supposed it was true that you had to see how it looked on the other side before you could appreciate what you had.

She hadn't really made this dinner. She'd called Ethan over, and he had made the dinner while she had helped him. Now she was reheating it and plating it as Ethan had said to. When the doorbell rang, Lydia jumped. Certainly, it wasn't time. She hadn't done her face up or anything. Looking at the clock, she saw it was indeed six o'clock, and her mother was punctual.

She took the scarf off of her hair and ran her fingers through it. She hoped it looked chic and messy. When she opened the door, her mother stood there.

Lydia was shocked.

Gone was Mayor Mason. For as long as Lydia could remember, her mother had lived in suits. Tonight, her mother had on a floral dress with floral sandals.

"I can tell from your expression that you weren't aware that I wore other kinds of clothes besides work clothes."

Lydia nodded. "You—You look beautiful. I mean, you always look beautiful, but tonight—"

It made Lydia feel a little self-conscious. She had on a pair of jeans and an off the shoulder white lace top that was embroidered with blue flowers on in it. She wasn't even wearing shoes. She hadn't found them yet. She stepped back and led her mother to the kitchen.

"I made spaghetti," Lydia said.

"Really? The last time I checked, your cooking skills were questionable. Questionable as in if we don't want to go to the hospital, we shouldn't eat it."

Lydia looked away and turned to the stove. She stopped when she felt her mother's hand on her shoulder.

"I'm sorry, Lydia. I wasn't trying to be mean. I just wanted you to know I do know some things about you."

Lydia looked up and stared at her mother. When she had made the first comment, Lydia felt each word as if it were a dagger. Then when she apologized, some of the sting went away. Lydia smiled.

"Well, let me alleviate your mind. I didn't make the spaghetti. I just assisted. Ethan made dinner for us, and he is an excellent cook."

"I'm glad to know we are in safe hands."

"Have a seat. One of the benefits of not having to really cook is that heating it up is a breeze." After she had finished heating it up, they both sat down for the meal. It wasn't long before the only sound that could be heard was the slurping of noodles and the chewing of food.

"Have you been out to the legal bar events lately?" her mother asked.

"No, the days the legal bar holds events are usually my late days for the legal clinic."

"I found out later on that your house is one the high schoolers are using for their contest."

Lydia smiled. "Yes, I've been a consistent member of the test group. It helps the kids, and it helps me. I don't worry about the yearly maintenance duties because they do them."

Mara nodded her head and smiled. They continued for another thirty minutes, and when dinner was over, the silence came back.

"Wow, this was harder than I thought it would be."

Mara nodded. "Is there nothing we can talk about? We are in the same office, and we work in the same field, but outside of work, certainly we have something to talk about."

Lydia could see her mother wanted to make an effort. She thought of Barrick and Ethan and decided if her mother wanted to make an effort, she could do no less.

"It's probably a good idea if we get to know each other."

Mara looked confused. "I know you already, Lydia."

Lydia looked at her mother and crossed her arms over her chest. "Okay, let's start there. What is it that you think you know about me?"

Mara smiled. "This is too easy. Are you sure you don't want to ask me a hard question?"

Lydia smiled. "I can see someone is very confident. Now I really want to know what it is you think you know about me."

"Okay, why don't we make it interesting? The first one who gets three wrong has to give something the other person wants. I can tell you what I want right now."

Lydia was intrigued by the game and by the dare that her mother thought she knew her.

"I'll bite. What is it you'd like as your prize if you win?"

"I want dinner with you once a week to get to know each other."

Lydia smiled. "You're already backing out. You said you knew me."

"I do. What would you like?"

"I'd like to talk about my dad."

Lydia saw Mara tense and then she breathed through. "Fine. Are you ready to play?"

Lydia nodded. "You're first?"

"I am. So, the rule is I go, and then you go until someone has lost."

"I'm good on the rule."

"The first thing I know about you, Lydia, is that you love chocolate."

Lydia smiled. "That is correct. I do love chocolate. I can match that one. So, the thing I know about my mother is that she also likes chocolate."

Mara made the sound of a beeper. "As it turns out, I am allergic to chocolate. I can't stand most sweets, and I especially can't stand chocolate."

Lydia's hands went to cover her face. She couldn't believe it.

"It can't be true. I spent years getting you the right chocolate for your birthday and for special occasions."

Mara didn't deny it. "You're right, but it just meant that I had to go out at night and find a lot of homeless people who would like to have some chocolate."

Lydia wrinkled her nose and thought on how many times people were so happy to see her. Now it was starting to make more sense on what was happening. Still, she wasn't the type of person to give up.

"Your turn."

Mara looked at Lydia and smiled.

"Your favorite color is blue."

Lydia wanted to ask if she had asked Yolanda. Instead, she nodded, and her mother smiled.

"I can see the look of suspiciousness on your face. No, I didn't have to ask your friends that question. When you were smaller, you would dress up your dolls, and they always wore blue. You didn't like red because it was too loud. You never liked any of the lighter colors either. You said they got too dirty too quickly."

Lydia looked at her mother and was confused. "I don't get it. How can you remember and know so much about me, but we've always had such a problem talking?"

Mara let out a big sigh. "The reason we have a huge problem talking is because we are so much alike. I know another thing about you. You will go with your gut every time when it's time to make a decision. You don't think about anything else. You'll make a decision with your gut even if the proof in front of you says not to do it."

Lydia didn't even bother to deny that one.

"I have to live with me. So, I go by my gut all the time. I guess you win because right now, I can't think of anything else that I think I know about you."

Mara nodded. She looked at Lydia, and it appeared to Lydia she was trying not to cry.

"You didn't win, but I was wrong. I shouldn't have made it so you didn't think you could ask about your father. He wasn't a bad man. He was exciting. He was bold, and he was all the things I was then."

"Then what happened?"

Mara laughed. "What happened is that one day we all have to wake up and realize it's time to be an adult. With it comes responsibilities. He wanted the adventure but didn't want to accommodate for the other changes that came with life. When you came, he gave me a choice, and I chose you."

Lydia gasped and tried not to say anything. She was too shocked with the news and the feeling that she had worshipped this man. She'd punished her mother for not letting her dad's name be spoken, and that thought was sitting at the front of her mind.

"I'm sorry. I think I'll be going now. I want you to know I won. So, I'll be expecting our weekly dinners. I know it's not my place. I know you don't see me like other kids do their mothers, but I want you to know I have your best in mind when I do things. When I saw you with Ethan, the first thing I thought was he wasn't your type."

"You don't know him."

Mara reached out and stroked her cheek.

"The problem is, I think I do, and I don't want you to get hurt."

"Hurt because he'll leave me?"

Mara shook her head. "No, I can say now that the leaving, when they do it, is the easy part. The hard part is when you discover that you've fallen in love with someone who doesn't love you the same way. With someone who won't stay by your side and fight with you. That's the part that hurts. It doesn't just hurt for the moment. It hurts for months. If I could, I would spare you that."

With those words, Mara gathered her items and left Lydia's house.

Lydia knew this was going to be a challenging evening. She knew Ethan was right and she had to deal with her mother, but this was more than she had expected. She thought about what her mother had gone through. She thought about how she had treated her mother, and guilt like she had never known dogged her steps as she cleaned up the kitchen.

Maybe her mother was right. She was right about some of those things. It didn't matter what proof was in front of her; if her gut said to go with it, she did. Her gut had okayed Ethan, and she had gone full speed ahead, but what did the facts say?

The facts said that Ethan was completely different from her. He had money. He grew up differently, and he had different experiences and customs that were setting off warning signs. As she washed the dishes, she remembered Barrick saying Ethan had hired Penny to work for him. Ethan hadn't mentioned it was someone from town. He also hadn't mentioned that the person he was taking on was a recommendation from his father; someone he had suggested.

Lydia hadn't even taken the time to look at what was going on with Ethan and his father. It didn't look like the two of them were going to be doing any reconciling any time soon. In fact, it looked like Ethan had resigned himself to being at odds with his dad.

What would happen if they decided to get together? What would happen if this went beyond dating and they had a full relationship? Would he be able to take the pressure of his father not accepting her?

There were so many questions and doubts rushing in on her now.

Lydia finished the dishes and stopped in front of the sink as the silence of the house settled over her. She crossed the kitchen and walked to her bedroom. She didn't look left or right but sank on her bed. She welcomed the down comforter and rolled into a ball under it.

She wasn't going to bawl her eyes out. She was determined to blink back the burning that was happening behind her eyes. She had to be stronger than this. She thought she knew what this was. She was so sure when she had spoken to Yolanda, but then her mother had reminded her about something very important tonight. Everyone had to agree with the definitions; otherwise, the definition didn't mean a thing.

Ethan knew something was wrong. For the past couple of days, he had reached out to Lydia, and she had given him excuse after excuse as to why they couldn't meet up. In fact, the only time he had even glimpsed her had been by accident.

He had seen her and Yolanda going for a juice, but he was having a meeting with Penny, trying to get her up to speed on how he did his work. She had seen him, waved, and then she and Yolanda had gone on their way. She hadn't even stopped to talk to him.

He tried to control his disappointment, but he had a business to attend to with Penny, and he said he would circle back and see what had happened. He knew something was wrong, but he couldn't pinpoint what it was. But he decided to give her some space. He was sure it was the dinner with her mother, and that was something he wanted her to work out.

Finally, he decided that he was going to address whatever it was this afternoon. After finishing his work at the Cades and leaving a list for Penny to do, he went to the courthouse. He found her office with no problem, and fate was on his side; she was alone. He could see what he assumed was Yolanda's purse, but she wasn't in the office.

"Hey stranger," he said jokingly.

"Yes, I am." She was still not his Lydia. Her response was dulled and off. He got ready to speak, but she stopped him.

Lydia took a deep breath and began. "I want you to know that you have been nothing but the best person in all of this. You didn't shy away from taking on my challenge of me showing you a better Sweet Blooms. And I hope I've done that."

Ethan nodded. "You have, and more. I was limited by my view on things, but that's been fixed now."

He expected that to get her going or at least to elicit a jibe at him, but it didn't. Something was very wrong.

"I think, after looking over everything, that this dating thing isn't such a good idea."

He didn't say anything. He had to listen to her complete whatever had gotten into her head.

"I think it was wrong of me to go ahead and even make the deal. You have a life, and I just barged in and made a proposition that was inappropriate."

"There weren't any complaints from me."

Ethan was listening to her, but what he was hearing was a Dear John, a thank you but it's over speech. He didn't understand what had happened. He thought they were on the same page. That they wanted the same things. Ethan knew how rare what they had was, and it was worth following no matter where it led. For once, Ethan didn't feel alone. He had someone to work with him. Maybe she didn't know, but he did. What they had was worth fighting for. Worth keeping.

"Really, this has gone on long enough, and we need to go our separate ways." She pushed forward with her explanation.

"Is that what the cold shoulder has been about for the last couple of days? You've been trying to find a way to tell me that you want me out of your life?" he demanded. Ethan looked around the office, he had such a feeling of impotence and anger with nowhere for it to go. Then he collected himself. He wasn't a child. He could think, and it was his brain that had gotten him out of more scrapes than he could count. What had changed?

"It's been a couple of days. What happened?"

The question brought her head up, and her eyes widened to twice their normal size.

"Tell me what happened with your mother and dinner. What did she say? You know our parents can be toxic. Why are you letting this happen?"

Lydia's face hardened, and she stood up. "You don't understand, and I have to tell you my relationship with my mother has gotten much better. We can talk, and I don't find her toxic, as you call it."

Ethan held up his hands in defense. "I'm sorry. I shouldn't have said toxic. I just meant our parents can be challenging."

Lydia opened her mouth and then let out a deep sigh. "This is just a cycle for you and me. We had some good times, and we make great friends, but I think if we really look at what we're doing, we'll find that maybe we aren't as compatible as we think. I was under the impression that we were dating and that this was still a part of the *feeling each other out* phase." She shook her head, "Is this how you act when things don't go your way? I think I'm being very clear. I'd like you to respect my wishes and understand. We live in a very small town, so if we can find a way to be polite to one another, there will be gossip, but it will blow over as long as we don't fan the flames with any antics."

Ethan could barely keep his voice together. He'd been here before. He understood not being good enough. He understood fear and rejection.

"I know how to keep myself together, so I won't embarrass you."

Lydia held up her hand. "That wasn't my insinuation. What I meant was—"

"Don't worry. I understood what it is that you meant. You meant that whatever we had between us is over. Don't worry, I get it."

He turned and almost ran over Yolanda. She looked like she had been caught with her hand in the cookie jar.

"Uh—" she started.

"No worries. I'll leave. It looks like you two have a lot to cover, and I'm just in the way," Ethan said as he walked by. He was walking away so he could figure out what was wrong. He was walking away to find a better plan. He hoped that she could eventually understand that they had found the love of a lifetime.

Lydia was lost in a sea of despair. Yolanda had tried to talk to her, but she couldn't speak so soon after Ethan had left. Instead, she threw herself into her work and tried to drown out the pain by not focusing on it. When the days passed and it was time to see her mother, she canceled. Seeing her made her think of Ethan even more.

Everywhere she looked she found Ethan, and it left her between holding back tears or falling into abject misery. It had been three days since she'd seen him. She knew what she had done was the best thing for both of them. She had, for once, looked at the evidence around them and made a logical decision.

She had seen him with Penny at the juice bar, and that had been the deciding factor. They looked happy together. Their heads had been close. Penny was what he needed. They worked together, and they had the same background. He wouldn't see it now, but it would be so clear to him later. She'd done the smart thing.

It might have been the smart thing, but it had ripped a hole in her whole being. Now that she understood what it was to connect to another person so completely, the loneliness was a pit of despair. She was so grateful for her career, as now it was her refuge from her feelings.

The worst was when she came home. She had remnants of Ethan all over. When she looked in the refrigerator, she saw the weird and unknown vegetables he'd left that he'd been planning to get her to try. When she sat on the couch, she saw the pillow he had helped her pick out. It said 'Couch potato, no way! Couch sitter certified!' She didn't want to throw the pillow away, but it was starting to act as a ward to keep her off the couch.

She knew she could call on Yolanda and she would come over. In fact, Yolanda had sent over a couple of texts to let her know that if she needed a friend, she could not only visit but also stay over. Lydia was grateful for the offer, but she didn't take it. She didn't think she'd be good company for her friend.

When dinner time came, she would think on both the conversations with her mother and with Ethan. She went back and forth between thinking maybe her mother was right and knowing she needed to have faith in her and Ethan.

There were times she could block him, but there was no doubt that the nights were the hardest. When she was in her bed and trying to get some sleep, all of the memories of what they'd done together came back to haunt her. They reminded her that Ethan was a good friend on top of everything else. He gave good advice. He appreciated what she could and couldn't do. He wasn't afraid to cook and be himself around her.

They were friends of a sort, and she felt the loss on two levels. He wasn't Yolanda, but she liked him as a person. He was a person she could trust. And if truth be known, Yolanda was right; he was definitely a good sight to look at.

All of that didn't matter because she had ended it. The best she could hope for was that somehow this gaping hole she had in her heart would heal and give her some peace.

It had been five very long days. Five days of not seeing Lydia. Five days of none of her humor. Five days of not seeing her be kind to everyone and putting herself last. In the last five days, Ethan had been doing some work.

He had visited her mother, the mayor. When he met Mara Mason at the juice bar and threw himself at her mercy, it wasn't pretty, and he had to admit that if she hadn't believed that he really loved her daughter, he wasn't beyond offering money. He had hoped it wouldn't come to that, but he knew he loved Lydia enough to be desperate enough to offer the money.

He went to see his dad. He wanted to be able to reconcile with him, but it was the same old thing every time. He had to do everything he wanted or it didn't count. When it came to money, he was open to listening, but when his father wouldn't listen about Lydia, they agreed to disagree. His father's argument always went back to what had happened between him and his mother, but he would never discuss exactly what had occurred.

Deciding to leave the past in the past, he did ask his father if he could accept Lydia, but he said it didn't matter if he did or not because Ethan was going to do what Ethan wanted. It wasn't the ending he wanted, but he had learned early in life, sometimes you didn't get what you wanted, and you needed to learn how to deal.

Now the last one was the most important one. If he couldn't get her on board then it would have all been for nothing. As the morning sun lit the path, he rang the bell at Lydia's front porch and hoped she would open. After ringing the bell for five minutes, the door was pulled open by a disheveled Lydia who looked like she was just getting out of bed.

"I'm so glad you opened up the door. It would have been really bad if I had to walk around the house tapping on windows to get your attention."

She pushed her hair out of her face and then looked at him. First, he saw the beginning of a smile starting to form on her face, but then it was dulled with a sadness that seemed to pull all of her happiness away.

"What are you doing here?"

Ethan held up a coffee box and a blue chocolate box. "Would it help our conversation at all if I tell you that, besides these gifts, I'm here with the full blessing of your mother?"

She didn't even reply; she just stepped back and let him enter. He went straight to the kitchen and put his goods down. He turned and saw she was standing in the doorway just looking miserable.

"I want you to know I had this long, scathing speech I was going to give you. It was about you not trusting us. It was about how we need to be able to talk to one another and not just run off with an idea and make decisions that will affect the both of us. I've been working on it for the last three days."

"Really?" she whispered. "I've been going to work and coming home like a zombie, thinking about how dull and lifeless my life would be without you in it. I've just been trying to find a way to bring up the subject that I was wrong, but I just didn't know how."

He walked towards her, and she went into his arms. He held her tightly and then took a deep smell of her hair.

"We can't let what happens to our parents decide what we are going to do. We're different people in a different time. I'm all for listening to them because I think they have something to say, but I don't think we can just go the way they went."

"Did you really talk with my mother?"

"Yes, I did. I realize now I probably should have talked to her as soon as I knew what I wanted."

Lydia pulled away from him.

"And you know what you want now?"

Ethan looked into her eyes, smiling.

"I've never been more sure. I'm thinking we'll start slow because you're cautious and all, and we can give it, say, two weeks. Then, after that, I'm thinking it'll be a good time to move on to getting engaged. Then, if everything is in order and all of the stars are aligned, I think I'll ask you to marry me. Then I'll do whatever it takes to make sure you say yes, and I'll spend the rest of my life making sure you are the happiest woman in the world."

He saw the tears rolling down her cheeks as Lydia smiled up at him.

"What does a woman say to all of that, Ethan?"

"To make sure I don't have a heart attack waiting? The correct answer would be yes."

Lydia's smile brightened.

"Yes, yes, yes!"

Epilogue

Adam Cade looked at his new business associate, Ethan Young, and was amazed at the transformation. It wasn't even a month ago that Ethan had approached him on how to help out Sweet Blooms.

When he had come to his office, he'd been dressed in an expensive suit, and the only promises he was making was that he would try to preserve the oldest members in the community. He wouldn't give any assurances for anything else.

Today he was in his office dressed in blue jeans, a white polo, and he was sporting a ring on his finger that every so often he would touch and look at. On top of that, Ethan was relaxed. His body wasn't as tense or as aggressive.

"So, I see being in love agrees with you," Adam said.

Ethan nodded. "Everything about her agrees with me. Even when we're not in agreeance, she still fits me. I have to tell you it's so comfortable to be with Lydia that I can't believe my good fortune."

Adam had been having some thoughts on the matter of his personal life. He wasn't sure he could even call it a personal life. It was more like a revolving door.

He was totally vested in his company, and when he was in a relationship, they expected him to change his priorities.

He had even gone so far as to find a woman who also liked to do woodworking. That had been a huge mistake. When they had first gotten together, it wasn't an issue, but as time went on she thought she would have some input on how Cade Designs was done. Even when he offered her a line all her own so she could create things unique to her brand, it wasn't enough. She wanted to decide what new things were going to happen in his company. When he told her no, she claimed he didn't trust her and left.

"I've been really impressed with the plans you have for Sweet Blooms, and if I'm not mistaken, it looks as though you're more vested in building it up than you were before."

Ethan smiled and fingered his ring at the same time.

"It's true. I've been speaking with Lydia, and we both agree that although we may have mixed feelings about the history of Sweet Blooms, it is still home and we want to invest in it so one day we'll be able to take our kids there."

Adam nodded. "I'm glad to hear that. I've made a decision to step down from Cade Designs. I'm not really needed here, and I want to be able to enjoy my life with a family."

Ethan nodded, understanding. "It's a big decision, but I'm sure you've thought it through."

Adam continued. "That's also why I've decided that I want to go home and find me a woman from Sweet Blooms."

Ethan stopped. "Excuse me?"

Adam nodded as if he was agreeing with himself. "I'll go to Sweet Blooms and find a good woman and then settle down."

"Uh, Adam, I think it's a little different with you."

"Why?"

"You're a millionaire."

"You've got money too Ethan."

Ethan gave him a level stare. "It's true, I have cash, but I haven't finished breaking up with what the world calls the most beautiful woman in the world. They'll all know your face and worth."

Adam dismissed it.

"You'll see. When I go home, they won't see my money. I go back twice a year. They'll see me, and I'll find a good woman. You'll see."

I hope you enjoyed *Sweet Attractions*. Check out *Sweet Beginnings* book two in the Love Happens Series and Hannah's story I've included Chapter One so you can start the adventure.

Sign up to my newsletter to receive updates on new releases, sale promotions, and free books.

susanwarnerauthor.com

Here's a peek at book 2

Sweet Beginnings

One

She was standing on a ten-foot ladder in a skirt with a shoebox hanging around her neck, with a bird inside.

"I can feel you hopping away in the box. When I get you next to the branch, you better hop on. I've got guests coming, and I don't need them to see little birdies who don't know how to stay in their nests."

Hannah Jenkins was cautiously making her way up the ladder, which leaned precariously against the house. This was just her luck. Today she was waiting for her first guests to come to her home. She needed some extra income and had decided this would be the way. If the city could make money on Airbnb, she could too.

It was all going well; she had picked out the perfect outfit for her brand-new guests. They were from New York, so she made sure she had on a skirt and blouse to look country chic. Then she heard it—the chirping of a baby bird. Hannah looked at the bird, and she was ashamed to say she thought about ignoring it. Then a vision of one of the cats prowling around the property came to mind. Hastily looking down the driveway, she started to think.

Looking up at the large tree next to the house, she saw the bird's nest in the "V" of the two branches that touched the side of the house. Did she have time? She needed this BnB thing to work. Trying to support a teen in a town without a lot of opportunities and an ex who had to be reminded to send support was hard. Then it happened again! The little bird chirped.

Hannah hurried to the side of the house to grab the compacted ladder. It took her twice as long to move it, as she was trying to make sure her skirt didn't get smudged. She knew she should have worn the dark skirt, but no, she wanted to look all delicate and floral. Hannah didn't have enough words to go over how ill-planned this was. She extended the ladder against the house and then reached for the bird, which promptly hopped away.

"You've got to be kidding me. I'm trying to help you!" Hannah exclaimed. Looking around, she saw a shoebox in the recycling, popped a hole in the top and through the bottom with her finger, threaded some recycling twine, and made a circle. She scooped the bird into the box, hung it about her neck, and then up the ladder she went. The bird hopped and chirped. "I know, little guy, almost there."

As if on cue, the adult birds returned, and none looked happy to see her coming toward the nest.

"I want you to know this is not a daily service," Hannah said, as she stood on the last rung of the ladder. She took the box from around her neck, opened the box, and the chick happily hopped back to the nest. That was when she heard wheels on gravel. She looked over her shoulder and just what she was trying to avoid was coming to pass. Her new guests were arriving, and she was on the ladder. Hoping to minimize the moment, she began to descend the ladder. An errant wind blew, ruffling her skirt. Hannah instinctively grabbed for her skirt to hold it down, and at the same time shook the ladder.

"I'm coming, don't move," someone called from below. "I'll steady it for you."

Hannah shook her head, trying to sort through all the acceptable answers as to why she would be on the ladder. "No worries, I've got it," she called out. "My timing is always off," she muttered to herself.

Hannah looked down and saw a man at the bottom of the ladder, and all she could think of was to hold the skirt tighter as she moved down. "Please step away from the ladder. I'm fine," she called out.

"It's no problem. I'm here," the man persisted.

"No, really, you should move away."

Hannah had slowed her descent as she realized the man wasn't moving. She was about to call out to the man, telling him to move aside so she could finish her descent without him knowing what color her underwear was, when another wind came. Then, like a perfect storm, it happened. Hannah bent down to gather more of her skirt. The ladder held firm, and her grip wasn't as tight as she thought. The next moment, though, the only thing she had in her grasp was her skirt.

It wasn't a far fall. It was even less of a fall because she never hit the ground. Instead, she fell into the firm grasp of the stranger who didn't know how to take basic instructions.

Hannah was cradled in the arms of what she could only deduce was one of her new renters. She released her skirt, tapped him on the arm, and he set her on her feet. As he put her on her feet, she couldn't help but notice the five foot eleven inches of him, giving him the perfect height to look into her eyes. Or how his arms didn't shake when she was in his arms, and at one hundred eighty pounds or the publicly disclosed one hundred and sixty, she wasn't a lightweight. When she braced her hand against his chest before he set her down, she didn't feel his heart thumping. She was thrilled. Injured people didn't make long staying guests.

"Excuse me. Are you okay?" she asked, smoothing her skirt down. She stood up to her full five feet eight inches and extended her hand. "Welcome to the Pearl B and—"

Hannah scrunched up her face and did a double take. This wasn't just any city renter. His face had been all over the tabloids not even six months ago. In the small town of Sweet Blooms, when one of our own hits the news, it was news for four months past the time it was news for everyone else. According to the town gossip, he was the spitting image of his father. The married women still spoke of how the Cade men had all been gifted with looks. They could have been models if it weren't for the fact, they all worked with their hands. He had the Cade trim beard, with the long eyelashes that would give the fake lashes a run for their money. Each one of their boys was named for someone in the Bible. It was said they needed it to balance out their sinfully good looks.

Adam Cade, Fortune 500 owner, and the man who walked away from the beautiful cover model Nadia Larson. The rumors ran rampant; what would make a man walk away from the most beautiful woman on the earth?

They had been photographed together, and he went from being an up and coming entrepreneur who was modernizing his family business and making the top 250 companies to watch, to being the man who would make perfect children with the perfect woman. Nadia Larson was the top model on both hemispheres. Adam brought a down-home quality that never went out of style. He didn't work out at the gym; he worked with his hands making furniture as his father had before him. If there was a picture of a country wholesome good guy, it would be Adam Cade.

Adam didn't forget his roots. He came to Sweet Blooms to bring business to the smaller ones in town. He always referred to his friends and business acquaintances to meet at Sweet Blooms. More importantly, when a natural disaster struck Sweet Blooms, he came and helped rebuild houses and invested money. They had never met before. No one wanted to speak to Henry Jenkins, and the woman who had been fool enough to marry him wasn't held in that high regard either. Adam Cade was the town hero, and he was here. She had just been caught by him.

It was a bit much. All her original insecurities started to flood back. This BnB thing had been a last resort. What if they didn't like her house? What if they didn't like the two rooms? This was Adam Cade; he had stayed in the best of the best, and he was coming to stay in her home for a week. What had she been thinking when she thought up this plan?

He smiled at her and held out his hand. "Thank you."

"For?" she asked, confused.

"I've never been able to introduce myself, as I'm the man who just saved you."

Hannah was transfixed watching his mouth move. She wasn't really into the bearded look, but she had to admit it looked good on him. Then his words penetrated the fog of male appreciation.

"Really? Well, you still can't."

His smile grew, and a perfect mouth was revealed. "I don't know. I seem to remember it a little different," he said, looking at her.

Hannah cocked her head to the side and folded her arms over her chest. "Let me tell you what really happened. I was coming down the ladder just fine when a man stood impolitely at the bottom of it and would not acknowledge common decency and move. Instead, he loitered at the bottom of the ladder, stopping me from getting down in a timely manner before the wind came."

"Ouch! I think I prefer my version better. Saving the helpless damsel in distress before she fell to her—"

"I wouldn't have needed saving if you had just moved! Now let's not squabble over the truth. You're here. Let's get you settled. How many bags do you have?"

He didn't move; he just stared at her, and for a moment she thought he had a sparkle from his white teeth. Okay, it was definitely time to move this along. She didn't have time for men. Besides, she had a talent for picking all the worst ones out of the bunch. So, Adam Cade may look like a shiny apple, but she knew there was something about him that was rotten to the core.

He held his hand out behind him. "I'll bring in the luggage. Let me introduce my grandmother, Delilah Cade."

"Welcome, Mrs. Cade," Hannah said, trying not to stare at the woman. You could tell she was older, but the Cade gene of good looks wasn't just on the male side. Hannah's mother had often cautioned her that she could never hide her thoughts.

Delilah Cade smiled and grabbed Adam's hand. She was the epitome of classic beauty and grace.

"I know my grandson means the best," Delilah said. "Forgive him. He's a do first and sort it out later kind of guy."

"It's no problem, gran," Adam said. "I'm sure Ms. Jenkins was glad I was here to assist."

Hannah had to clench her teeth to let the moment of frustration pass by. She warred with telling him what she really thought and not having to break the news to Delilah Cade, who looked at her grandson with such love and devotion, not even she had the heart to let her know the truth.

"I'm sure Mr. Cade had the best of intentions. However, I really will have to ask that he try to control his take charge inclinations. Things are a little different out here, and I want to make sure he stays safe."

Adam laughed. "I have to say that this is a first for me. I think you're trying to put me in my place."

Hannah smiled at him. "All of us mortals have this experience. I'm sure you, too, will adjust."

"Thank you for the lesson, Hannah. Not many people disagree with me when I'm right."

"Right?" She took a deep breath.

"Why don't we move on. Follow me, and I'll show you to your rooms."

She slowed her pace to make sure Mrs. Cade wasn't rushed. She was so conscious of the warm, deep tones of his voice as he spoke to his grandmother. She could see his shadow in front of her. Was everything about him impressive? She really needed to focus.

She knew she had a rotten apple to the core pick-a-man syndrome. If she was looking for someone, and she wasn't, but if she were, it wouldn't be with super famous Adam Cade. She would like someone who had some very specific characteristics. He would have to be happy with her baby, Nathan, who wasn't really a baby anymore. He was about to become a teen without a dad. She would also be looking for someone who would be happy with her. Is Adam Cade happy with her? That was a non-starter. A man didn't rebound from the most beautiful woman in the world to be with plain jane and her son. Adam would find his new Nadia because Barbie always found Ken.

Hannah had learned a lot about herself since her split with Henry. She knew that she could depend on herself to provide for herself and her son. She knew she was strong, determined, and had a quick mind. She also knew her hobby of making quilts and blankets was a budding business that would provide for her and her son. She was self-sufficient. She also knew the town of Sweet Blooms had some small-minded people. While most of the residents were understanding, there were some who didn't think the divorced wife of Henry Jenkins should be living on the Jenkins farm. It didn't matter to them that Henry hated it. She had been judged a golddigger who had stolen Henry's land in the divorce. As an owner of one of the original tracts of land in Sweet Blooms, she was grandfathered to the council, but that hadn't endeared her to anyone either.

She had spent a lot of time trying to get accepted by

the town. Not for her sake, but for Nathan's. He was going to go to high school next year, and he had enough problems without being reminded his mother was an outsider and, by default, so was he.

"Ms. Jenkins?"

"Yes?" she snapped.

Hannah had been so far in her thoughts she had walked them to their room and was standing in the doorway. "I see these are two adjoining rooms and the bathrooms are inside like the brochure says. Is there anything else you wanted to show us or house rules?"

She shook her head wildly. "No, no. I'm so sorry."

"It's no problem. You've had a harrowing day." Adam grinned at her and leaned against the door in front of her. "I'll see you tonight?"

Tonight? she repeated to herself. *That's right!* Mr. rotten somewhere at his core was living here for the week. She would provide room, board, and two meals a day—breakfast and dinner. "Of course, I'll see you later."

She heard Delilah call out, "I'll see you later, dear."

"Of course, I'll see you later," Hannah replied.

She stepped away from the door without acknowledging Adam anymore. When the door was closed, Hannah looked to the heavens and couldn't believe the way she had acted. She had to get dinner together. Maybe having a different focus would help her not focus on Adam Cade.

Cooking was dependable, she thought. It was a set of clear instructions held together by order and then executed in such a way that practically guaranteed a satisfying result. But men—they didn't seem to comprehend the word dependable. Looking at the way

Adam had left Nadia, dependable might be a foreign word for him too. For a moment, when she came down from the ladder, and she was in his arms, she felt safe and treasured.

It wasn't the chemistry that couples are built on. It was the hint of something that could be. Almost a taste of what might be. Even Hannah had to admit it felt good. The bad news was it was happening with her guest. Her guest had dumped the most beautiful woman in the world. He was so way out of her league.

In Adam's world of perfection, she didn't even exist. She would never be given a second look because she was honest enough to know she was attractive, but she didn't stop men in their tracks. The real problem she found was she was too trusting, and she believed in love. Believed in putting in the work through sickness and health.

Shaking off her maudlin thoughts and concentrating on dinner, she was able to bring her mode back up. Fashion came and went; maybe a good woman who wanted to stand by a man and support him would come back in style too. Until Mr. Ordinary showed up, she'd better make sure she was self-sufficient and could take care of her son.

Adam had put away the luggage and had taken a walk around the house. It was a five-bedroom home that seemed like it would be more suited for a large family than a bed and breakfast. The floors had been recently waxed, and the railing on the staircase was shining.

However, other little things told him all was not as

new as she wanted it to be. If he looked hard enough, he could see her attempts to hide what he thought was damage to the house. The connecting door between the rooms at first glance looked like it was there for guest convenience, but he could see how the paint was a little darker around the door than the rest of the room. The blue was a good color to use, but he could still see the signs of water damage. If he had to guess he'd say that the door was installed as a way to hide some leaking pipes, and Ms. Jenkins hadn't been able to quite find a perfectly matching blue paint.

As he walked through the house, the builder in him could see it had great bones. This was a house he could happily spend some time renovating.

On the side of the house was a garden that had been fenced off and a small, cushioned bench sat inside the perimeter. That was where he was going to take his grandmother. He'd been thinking about his life since the breakup with Nadia, and he needed a change. An idea had been forming in his head for that change and he'd recently formed a plan to start a new career in Sweet Blooms. He had carefully thought over his plan to start a new venture in Sweet Blooms and he looked at others who had done the same thing.

Now that the time was at hand and he could see his grandmother coming around the corner, he was nervous. Grandma Delilah was a spitfire to be sure. She was also the most level-headed person he knew and the one person whose opinion mattered to him more than anything. She was also the one person who supported him no matter what.

When Adam's father found out he wanted to join the family business, he had told Adam no. Daniel Cade said he wanted better for his son than to be a laborer. His grandmother had recognized his talent and got him into an apprenticeship.

When his father passed away, his grandmother had been his rock. When his sister and brother thought it was better to sell the struggling company, his grandmother had stood by him to keep it and make it grow. Now, Designs by Cade was known throughout America and they had so many requests in the pipeline that they had to turn business away.

He had done his duty by his family and made sure they were provided for and happy in their business. He had groomed his sister Corinne to take over because she was good at taking charge on a higher level. His brother Luke didn't thrive in the office. He enjoyed doing the designs and couldn't stand being in meetings every day so Adam left him alone to his designs.

Now Adam was ready to do something for himself.

The last fiasco with Nadia had brought it to bear that it was time for him to live his life. The rumors about their breakup got more fantastic as time went on. In truth, Nadia broke up with him. She wanted it to leak that he had left her because she needed some sympathy to boost her career. Nadia was a lovely woman, but he wanted one that would just be happy being with him. Nadia was happy as long as he wanted to be in the limelight with her.

He always enjoyed coming back to Sweet Blooms. Over the years he had made friends here and helped people. Some of those people had even come to call him Delilah's Boy. He couldn't think of a reason gran would say this wasn't a good idea, but until it was done, it was still up in the air.

"I've been waiting on you, gran," he said, holding out his hand to her. When she put her hand in his, it felt so warm. It was just one more sign of how nervous he was. In the end, he'd do what the best thing for him was, but if she didn't agree, he'd be less for it. His gran had been the one to always support him through thick and thin.

"I see something is weighing on you," she said.

"I was glad when you wanted to come here to get away for your birthday. It's like it was a sign," he started.

"Hmm, go on." She eyed him knowingly.

"I've decided that I want to step down from the company. I want to start to live a normal life. The company is set up so Corinne can run it. Luke will still do designs. They don't need me there anymore, and I need to move on." He said it in one breath, and suddenly, the load was off his chest.

"If you made up your mind, why are we out here?"

Adam laughed. "Because I wanted to know your thoughts. Having two made-up minds is better than one."

She shifted on the bench. "All the cushions in the world won't make this bench comfortable. You should give her some dead stock on the old treated pieces."

Adam smiled. Gran could throw a curve ball at you while she thought on things.

"Well, I have some questions."

"I thought you would."

"Did you decide you wanted to walk away because you're running from Nadia?"

"Ouch, gran! I'm not running. I will say the whole event helped me to see what I really wanted, and how it wouldn't really be possible on the road I was on."

His grandmother turned to him and pulled him into her arms.

"I'm so glad you're looking out for you because I was starting to worry," she said. "You know I'm beyond proud of you. Besides that, I'm not getting any younger, and I'd like to see some of my great-grandchildren."

"I don't even have a wife, and you're looking for grandchildren."

"Goals, boy, you have to set goals," she laughed. "When and where would you be making this great exodus?"

"I wanted to move here to Sweet Blooms."

Delilah laughed out loud and patted her chest to catch a breath. "You do know that all the women in this town will be flocking to you in no time."

"I'm not going to tell everyone. I'm going to take my time and not make any public announcements, to avoid the publicity."

Delilah patted him on the leg. "Boy, you may know the city, but you don't know small towns. If you stay here long enough, you'll find that people find out what's going on almost as quickly as you think it."

"Ah-hem, I'm sorry to interrupt, but dinner is ready if you are?" A soft voice said behind them.

Adam and Delilah turned to see Hannah at the gate. Delilah smiled at Adam. He wanted to ask her what the smile was for, but she brushed him off and said she had to get to supper, or they'd offend Hannah.

Later that evening, Hannah went out to her garden—trying to find some peace from the day—when her cell phone rang. Five minutes later, she regretted not ignoring the phone.

"You have got to be kidding me," Hannah said on her cell. Shaking her head in disbelief, she walked out the back door and into the garden. She grabbed her pink foam knee pad and shook the loose dirt from it. She could tell she'd need a relaxing distraction in order to get through this phone call. She picked up a pitcher and dropped water over her garden tools to make sure they were clean.

"Hannah, I am dying! I need to stay in the hospital for a little longer," the voice on the other end of her headphone whined. Hannah grabbed the shovel, rinsed it, and then put it back in her kit.

"We're all dying, Henry. Your son is waiting here for you to come this week. You promised!"

"The hospital won't let me out."

"Okay, which hospital are you in?" Hannah was so tired of his excuses. The only thing she could focus on was how Nathan was going to be disappointed again.

"Well, I wouldn't want to put anyone out. It's no place to see a man in." Henry stammered and backpedaled as he tried to bolster his thin excuse.

"Tell me, Henry, what new opportunity is going on?" She bit out each word, trying not to let the bitterness or the held back tears, seep into her voice.

"The city is a great place, Hannah. You always think it's the city that's coming between us. I can't help it if the city has these great work opportunities for me. I don't understand why you stay in Sweet Blooms anyway. There's nothing here for you. All the opportunity for you can be found in the city. Think about what the income could do for you and Nathan."

She wouldn't argue with Henry about how great he thought the city was. When it came to choices, the city always won. It was more important than her, and it was more important than their son Nathan.

Exhausted with it all, she sat back on her haunches and looked at her faded denim jeans.

"Henry, are you coming, yes or no?"

"No, I can't. I told you—"

"Fine, when are you going to tell Nathan?"

"Well, I don't know when the hospital will let me on the phone again. So maybe it would be best if you told Nathan. I-I mean, I'll try, but just in case, make sure you tell him."

"Henry! No, I—"

"Hey, I gotta go. Thanks, Hannah."

The next moment she was listening to the dial tone. She dropped the cell in her pocket and tried not to imagine how her son would take the news when he returned home in a couple of days.

Made in the USA
Columbia, SC
19 October 2021